Seduced by a SEAL

AN ALPHA SEALS NOVEL

Makenna Jameison

ISBN: 9781729475720

Table of Contents

Chapter 1	1
Chapter 2	16
Chapter 3	31
Chapter 4	39
Chapter 5	49
Chapter 6	58
Chapter 7	65
Chapter 8	71
Chapter 9	77
Chapter 10	84
Chapter 11	91
Chapter 12	99
Chapter 13	104
Chapter 14	113
Chapter 15	115
Chapter 16	121
Chapter 17	134
Chapter 18	141
Chapter 19	149
About the Author	159

Chapter 1

Colton "C-4" Ferguson grumbled under his breath as the security line at Miami International Airport inched forward. He shifted his duffle bag onto his broad shoulder and took a swig from his bottle of water before tossing it into the nearby trashcan. Scrubbing a hand across his jaw, he blew out an irritated sigh as the woman at the front of the line pleaded with the TSA agent to let her keep the iced coffee she was holding.

Good grief.

Like she couldn't just buy another drink once they cleared the TSA checkpoint.

Glancing at his watch, he wondered if he'd be able to intercept the target before catching his flight back to Little Creek. It wasn't exactly the usual Navy SEAL MO to go after an individual on U.S. soil, but he'd happened to be down in Miami on R&R when his CO had notified him that a high-value asset was flying out of the airport at the same time he was.

Colton had immediately agreed to assist and garner any intel he could.

Hell, he'd miss his flight if need be. Anything to make their upcoming op run smoother.

After a brief meeting with some guys who wouldn't say what agency they were from, he'd gotten some small electronic devices to bug the target's belongings. The men he'd met with had assured him they wouldn't set off the airport metal detectors.

And naturally, he'd picked the slowest moving line on Earth. It wouldn't do him a hell of a lot of good to be in the airport at the same time if he was stuck in the damn security line while she hopped on her flight and flew out of the country.

The crowded airport and never-ending lines almost made him miss the naval base hangars and C-17 cargo planes his SEAL team flew on. Almost. Because sitting in an uncomfortable seat, headphones on to drown out the noise on a nonstop flight across the Atlantic wasn't exactly a vacation. Then again, not dealing with the TSA and travelers insisting on doing things their own way made up for the discomfort, he thought with a smirk.

A toddler cried in line in front of him, her mother looking frazzled as she attempted to haul her little girl, luggage, and baby gear forward as the line finally moved.

"I got it," he said, easily lifting the car seat she was pulling around the airport onto the conveyor belt to go through the x-ray machine. He dropped his own duffle bag down beside it before toeing off his boots and putting them alongside his watch, wallet, and cell phone in the bin.

An overstuffed diaper bag and collection of

blankets and stuffed animals filled the bin in front of his. And that was in addition to the car seat and luggage the woman had.

Hell.

At least being single he could travel light.

The young mom shot him a grateful look, anything she said as she tried to thank him drowned out by her child's cries.

Colton's gaze swept around the other lines: an elderly couple was inching along, holding up the line to his left. Three teenagers were laughing hysterically on the other side of them as one girl jumped up and down, trying to put her shoes back on. A few business travelers shot annoyed glances at the cell phones, irritated by the entire scene.

And then his eyes locked on a stunning woman two lines over.

She had long, dark hair, skin the color of smooth caramel, and curves that would make a grown man weep. The sexy little red sundress she had on barely covered her nicely rounded ass, and he admired the swells of her breasts as she turned to the side, hands animatedly flying around as she argued with the TSA agent.

"It's just cleanser," she said, throwing her arms up in exasperation. Her voice carried over the people around him, and Colton noticed a slight Colombian accent. "It's for washing my face—add a little water and scrub. Want me to demonstrate?"

The TSA agent looked unamused and radioed for backup. A female agent guided the gorgeous woman aside for a pat down, and Colton felt his cock swell as he took in her shapely form. His chest tightened as he watched the female agent's gloved hands move over the mystery woman's ribcage and hips.

Instantly, his protective instincts surged.

He didn't want some strange woman touching her.

Hell.

He didn't want *anyone* touching her.

Except maybe him.

At that moment, he'd never wanted to be a TSA agent so badly in his life. Never mind that the monotony of standing around in an airport all day was nothing compared to the life and career of a Navy SEAL. He'd never envied someone so much as he watched the female agent pat her down.

The woman in the red sundress pouted in exasperation as the other agents examined the container that had been brought into question, and Colton drank in her red lips, high cheekbones, and chocolate brown eyes. She caught him watching her for a split second, her fiery gaze almost daring him to do something, but then her eyes landed back on her luggage.

"I already told you there's nothing in my luggage that could be considered harmful."

"Next!" the agent in Colton's line called out.

Colton's eyes swept back to him, and he stepped forward, handing over his ID and boarding pass.

The photograph he'd tucked into his pocket was slightly grainy, but there was no mistaking her. The woman he was targeting was stuck in security just like him.

His jaw ticked as he saw two officers with bomb-sniffing dogs now converging on the scene.

How exactly was he supposed to bug her belongings if she was intercepted by airport authorities?

The woman began rapidly talking again, looking more and more irritated. Colton cleared the metal detectors and grabbed his gear from the bin, sliding his phone and wallet back into his pockets and putting on his boots in haste. His metal watch went back around his wrist, and then he was grabbling his duffle bag and dodging other travelers to get to the woman.

"It's an exfoliator," she said in exasperation to the bomb techs.

"A what?" one of the men asked, holding the container up for closer inspection with gloved hands.

"A cleanser. For washing my face. I already explained it earlier—you add water to it. People use soaps and cleansers, no?"

Colton opened his mouth, ready to speak, when the dumbfounded agent to the right glanced up. His eyes widened in recognition when he noticed Colton heading their way. "C-4!" he said with a grin.

He stepped aside and held out a hand to Colton. "What're you up to, man? Visiting Miami? It's been years!"

Colton shook hands with the man he'd gone through explosives training with many years ago. "Headed back to Little Creek," he said, unable to prevent his gaze from drifting back toward the stunning woman. "Just here for a little R&R."

"Well shit. I could go for a vacation."

Colton chuckled. "Our entire team got some time off after our most recent op. It was hell, so we all appreciated the break. Probably won't get another breather for a while. You know how it is—on duty 24/7, at Uncle Sam's beck and call."

"Understood. Can't say I miss life in the military at

all. You know her?" he asked, watching the scene around them. The woman had backed away from the agents and was mouthing off to them, her hands on her hips as she tapped her foot impatiently on the ground.

Colton's eyes slid back up her toned legs, appreciating the curve of her ass, and quickly skimmed over her full breasts before he eyed his buddy again. "Not yet."

His buddy laughed. "She's a handful. Probably harmless. Don't know what the hell she's got in that container though. I've never seen powdered soap before. Face wash. Whatever the hell she claims it is."

"Women," Colton said with a smirk. "They can line the entire bathroom counter with beauty products and still need something new. A good old bar of soap works just fine for me."

"She looks high maintenance all right. Pretty damn fine though," he chuckled.

"All right, ma'am," one of the agents testing the woman's luggage said. "You're free to go. Next time consider checking that in your luggage."

"It's about time," she said, flipping her long, dark hair over her shoulder and nailing him with a glare. "I nearly missed my flight thanks to you."

"It's standard procedure, ma'am," the agent replied. "Anything brought into question needs to be fully inspected."

"Standard. Right," she said in her Colombian accent. "I think you just wanted a chance to pat me down. Thankfully another woman did the job instead," she added, her voice doing strange things to Colton's libido. "I certainly don't need your hands all over me."

Colton smirked.

Hell.

Another man on their Delta SEAL team, Hunter "Hook" Murdock, had just ended up with a British chick he'd rescued while in London. She'd been on the run from terrorists, and Hunter, along with their teammate Mason "Riptide" Ryan, had just happened to be in the right place at the right time. He'd rescued her from a pub, and they'd temporarily holed up in a hotel room together.

And the rest was history.

The fact that his rough-and-tumble friend, the guy who once practically had a different woman in his bed every night, was now in a committed relationship had their entire SEAL team ribbing him.

What were the chances that Colton would be practically drooling over a woman who wasn't American either?

Not that he planned on settling down with the daughter of a notorious drug lord. Or settling down period.

Hunter's woman, Emma, had ended up moving to the U.S. with him. The woman Colton was eyeing in the sexy red dress very clearly intended to get on the next flight back to Colombia. He wished he didn't have to make a run for his own flight after his brief intercept. Wouldn't he love to buy her a stiff drink at the airport bar and let his gaze linger on her sumptuous curves. Long, sexy legs. Full breasts. Curvy hips.

Hell. He'd be sporting a hard-on all the way to the gate at this rate.

Still, he couldn't resist but to linger around as she collected her things. He could easily be on his way, but where would the fun in that be?

His buddy called out goodbye as he moved off toward another line needing bomb techs.

"Going my way?" Colton asked the gorgeous brunette, nodding the direction he was headed. "Maybe I could give you a hand with your luggage."

"Not unless you're headed to international departures," she said, those chocolate brown eyes twinkling with mischief.

"I could make a detour," he suggested.

"And what makes you think I'd want your company?" she asked seductively, her eyes raking over his torso. As a Navy SEAL, Colton was in excellent shape. He was used to women staring at him and his teammates everywhere they went. But something about this particular woman set him on fire.

Her dark eyes skimming over his broad shoulders, chiseled abdomen, and very pointedly landing below the belt as she eyed his package felt almost as if she were running her hands all over him.

And hell if he wouldn't love to make that a reality.

His cock twitched as she licked her red lips and innocently glanced back up at him.

If only he had a few hours to kill.

Hell. He wouldn't mind a few *days* alone with this woman. Exploring her curves. Moving over her gorgeous body. Teasing and tasting and caressing her everywhere until she was crying out beneath him.

Making her beg for release.

Colton chuckled. "I've never had any complaints before. And with the way you were eyeing me a moment ago, I thought you might be interested."

She laughed, a low, husky sound, and instantly his

groin tightened. The last woman he'd dated was more of a girl than a woman—innocent. Inexperienced. Willing to let him take the lead both in and out of the bedroom. He had a feeling this woman knew her way around a man's body. Hell, he'd happily let her take control if it meant a night in his bed.

A loud crash of thunder sent his gaze flickering toward the far windows in the airport terminal as the woman at his side jumped in surprise. Pouring rain began hitting the glass sideways, the wind whipping leaves around, and Colton muttered a curse.

He might just get his wish after all—hours alone with nothing to occupy his time but this woman.

The loudspeaker crackled a moment later. "Attention all passengers," a female voice said. "All flights in and out of Miami International Airport have been canceled until further notice due to the severe weather conditions. I repeat, attention all passengers—"

"Unbelievable," the woman in the red sundress exclaimed, throwing her hands up in the air. Colton caught sight of her manicured nails, painted a bright shade of red. She began speaking rapidly in Spanish as Colton watched in amusement.

"Let me buy you a drink," Colton suggested, his voice low. "Unless you have other plans?"

"I have no other plans at the moment, as you clearly can see. This was the last flight to Colombia today. It's not like I can catch a cab there. I'm stuck here until the flights are no long grounded."

"I promise I'm good company," he said with a wink. "Come on." He reached over and grabbed her bags, slinging her large tote over his own duffle bag. He picked up her sleek suitcase and, turning away, left her little choice but to follow him.

"Let me guess. You're some kind of athlete or something?" she asked, eyeing his arms before meeting his gaze as she walked along beside him. "American football player? Another sport?"

"Something like that," he said, the corner of his mouth quirking up in a smile.

He'd tell her he was military later on. Maybe. No point in explaining that he was a Navy SEAL. Not when he knew who her father was. She'd be running as fast as she could in the other direction. It wasn't exactly a secret that SEALs deployed on ops all over the world. Maybe she couldn't care less, assuming her father and his cartel thought they were above the law—but he sure as hell had no reason to bring it up.

Maybe he'd try to talk her into getting a hotel room with him after they'd had a few drinks—assuming they were in fact stranded for the night.

He'd see what information he could find out about her father. Bug her suitcase and other bag with the small electronic transmitters he'd acquired.

And the fact that she was fucking gorgeous?

A one-night-stand with her in his bed suited him just fine.

"Let's grab a table at the bar over there. The place will be packed soon now that all flights have been canceled. Hopefully it'll only be a couple of hours until they allow air traffic in and out again, but you never know. We could be here all night."

"Well aren't you a master at planning ahead," she said, tossing her long hair over her shoulder.

"A master?" he asked with a smirk.

She rapidly began speaking in Spanish again, and he assumed it was some sort of insult. It was hard to complain though with the way his groin tightened as he watched her.

"Easy," he said with a grin. "I just like to have a game plan."

"A game plan. See? You do sound like a professional athlete."

Colton chuckled. "Nope. My plan is pretty damn simple though—drinks at the airport bar, grabbing a room for the night."

Those chocolate brown eyes met his. "I suppose you have a hotel room already reserved as well? Just in case?"

"That's not a bad idea," Colton agreed, grabbing his phone from his pocket. He stopped mid-terminal and swiped the screen to unlock it.

"You're reserving a hotel room?" she asked, her mouth dropping open.

"You don't have to stay with me," Colton said with a chuckle. His eyes heated. "Not unless you want to that is. I wouldn't turn down the company of a beautiful woman. But it sure beats sleeping on a bench in the airport, right?"

She blew out a sigh. "No, that sounds less than comfortable. Should I be reserving a room for myself, too?"

"Only if you want. As I already said, you're more than welcome to spend the night with me."

He swiped a few things on the screen, and a moment later he tucked his phone back into his pocket.

"Just like that?"

Colton shrugged. "Better safe than sorry. There's supposed to be thunderstorms all afternoon and evening. My guess is that we're here until morning."

"Wonderful," she muttered. "I knew I should've taken an earlier flight. I probably wouldn't have been stopped by security either."

He smirked as she started walking toward the bar across the concourse, her hips swaying back and forth as she moved. In a few long strides he was beside her again. Colton guided her to a small bar-height table, leaving her suitcase and their bags at his feet. Without asking, he reached over and wrapped his large hands around her hips, helping her up onto the barstool.

She bristled slightly at his touch, but he didn't miss the intake of her breath as he got close to her. Or the exotic floral scent she was wearing.

Hell.

The woman was gorgeous. And as she crossed her long legs, he noticed she wasn't wearing a dress like he first thought, but some type of shorts outfit.

"Something wrong?" she asked, looking at his confused expression.

"I thought you had on a dress," he said, his eyes sliding back up over her body until he met her amused gaze.

"It's a romper," she said, pressing her lips together as she tried not to laugh.

"A what?"

"It's the latest fashion."

Colton blew out a breath, shaking his head in disbelief. "I can't keep up with women sometimes."

"You don't like it?" she asked, crossing her legs and then smiling as his gaze landed on her bare thighs.

Hell. She was gorgeous. "I like it too much," he said. "It hugs your curves perfectly."

She threw her head back and laughed, that long

12

brown hair tousling around her shoulders. "That's the idea. It's meant to flaunt a woman's best assets. It got your attention, no?"

Colton settled onto his own barstool, his gaze meeting hers. "It works for me. But hell, with a gorgeous body like yours, I'd imagine you'd look good in anything. Or even nothing at all," he added suggestively.

"If I'm going to allow you to buy me a drink, don't you think you should tell me your name?"

"Colton Ferguson," he said, holding out a hand. Her soft, feminine hand slid into his, and he resisted the urge to tug her even closer as his fingers wrapped around hers.

"Camila," she said.

Colton raised his eyebrows.

"Just Camila for now," she said in her Colombian accent.

"All right, Just Camila," he said, lightly running his thumb over her knuckles before letting her go.

"A woman can't be too careful," she said with a shrug. His gaze dropped to her full breasts as they rose and then fell again with her movement.

"You won't get any complaints from me," he assured her. "Tell me your name, don't tell me your name. It's all good. What can I get you?"

"I'd love a shot of Aguardiente. I doubt they have it though," she added with a husky laugh.

"What's that?"

"A Colombian liquor. Perfect to have a couple of shots of before you go out dancing."

"No, I don't think they serve that here," he said in amusement, crossing his arms. Her red lips pursed in a hint of a smile. His cock hardened as her appreciative gaze slid over his biceps.

"Ah. Figures." Her gaze flickered around the bar area. Tables were filling up, much as Colton predicted. A woman the next table over was speaking loudly on her cell phone trying to find a hotel room.

Camila caught his eye, raising her eyebrows.

"I told you so. Give it an hour or so and every hotel room around here will be booked." He glanced down at his watch. "If you prefer, we could have drinks back in my hotel room where it's a little quieter."

"And what makes you think I'd want to accompany a man I just met to his hotel room?"

"You tell me, kitten. You've been eying me with interest for the past ten minutes."

"Kitten? More like a tiger," she said with a scowl.

Colton chuckled, his deep laughter filling the room. "More like a tiger cub," he said, his eyes heating. "One I'd very much like to tame."

"All right," she said, preparing to slide off the high barstool. Colton instantly moved closer, his hands wrapping around her hips as he easily lifted her down. Her breasts brushed against his hard chest, and he resisted the urge to groan in appreciation. Unable to miss the chance to hold her close, he let his hands span her narrow waist, his fingertips just skimming over the top of her curvy ass.

"You're beautiful," he said, finally releasing her.

She laughed. "I already agreed to go with you to your hotel room."

"Ah, but the night is still young."

"Are you going to be a gentleman and carry my bags?" she asked, her gaze landing at the pile of luggage on the ground.

"Absolutely," he said, his voice gruff. His eyes locked with hers.

"Let's have champagne sent to the room," she said, wrapping her arm around his forearm and cozying up next to him.

"Champagne instead of Aguardiente. I can do that," he said with a low chuckle.

"It's more romantic," she said, her dark eyes darting toward his. "Drinking in a bar is different than a hotel room, no?"

Colton grabbed their bags, letting his arm wrap around her waist to pull her closer. "It certainly is. This way, kitten," he said, guiding her toward the door. "I'd love to have a bottle of champagne with you."

Chapter 2

Camila's gaze flicked around the busy airport as they walked out, Colton's large frame an imposing figure at her side. He towered over her, well past six feet. Even with her wedge espadrilles on, she only came up to his shoulder. He had muscles upon muscles and looked as if he trained hard every day. With his short, dark hair and gaze that didn't miss a thing, she wondered what exactly he did. He was alert and aware of their surroundings—a man used to commanding a room. Garnering attention wherever he went.

Blinking lights on the arrivals and departures board caught her eye. There was nothing but a list of flights followed by the word "Delayed."

Lovely.

Even if they did reopen the airport, it could be hours before her own flight was rescheduled. Another crack of thunder boomed, and the rain was coming down so hard she could hear it pounding outside as they approached the front of the airport. A separate set of doors led to an attached hotel, and she was grateful she wouldn't need to run out in the pouring rain.

Her father would have a fit that she wasn't arriving home from Miami today as scheduled, but what was she supposed to do?

Air traffic control grounding flights in and out of the airport was one of the few things out of his control.

The head of the notorious Rodriguez Cartel in Bogota, Miguel Rodriguez certainly had the means and connections to hire a private jet and get his daughter back to Colombia. But that would mean she'd let him know of her change in plans—which she certainly wasn't about to do.

Miguel always had to be one hundred percent in command and control. And maybe his goons were more than happy to acquiesce, to practically fall at his feet when he snapped his fingers, but Camila?

She'd never been one to let him control her life.

Not now and not ever.

She shuddered, thinking of the poor women that had been drawn into the kidnapping ring that funded his massive drug operation. The women were snatched from the streets. Held in small cells. Sold to the highest bidder. Cocaine production was back on the rise in Colombia thanks to her father. No doubt it was making its way north to the U.S.

And the women whose lives were stolen from them?

There wasn't a damn thing she could do to help.

"Are you okay?" Concern was etched in his gaze as she looked up at him.

Her eyes ran over his strong features—broad

forehead, warm brown eyes, full lips, and a strong jaw covered in a few days' worth of stubble. She may not know the man, but she felt that she could trust him. Be safe with him. Colton didn't give her the leering looks that some of her father's henchman did. They'd never touch her because of who *he* was, of course.

But if something ever shifted the dynamic in power?

She'd be thrown to the wolves. Tossed around from man to man until there was nothing left of her.

Colton's strong presence gave her a different feeling of security. His warm, hard body beside her, holding her close, left her mind reeling. She was going to go spend the night with the man, not live with him happily ever after.

The fact that he made her comfortable in a way she never had been was irrelevant.

"I'm perfect," she assured Colton. "Just thinking of my father." He raised his eyebrows as she laughed. "Nothing worth discussing, I assure you. He'll probably be wondering where my flight is since I was scheduled to arrive home this afternoon." She gave a careless shrug as his gaze dropped to the movement of her breasts. "It doesn't concern me, so there's no need for it to concern you."

"If you say so," he said, pushing open the door to the luxury hotel attached to the airport, his lips quirking up on one side.

She smiled as she stepped through the door. "Were you here in Miami on vacation?"

"Yep, just for a few days. I was catching a flight back home, hoping to beat the storm."

She playfully pouted at him. "And were you still hoping for a quick departure after you spotted me?"

He chuckled, and the deep sound of his laughter made her stomach do a funny little flip. She didn't date men—and not only because of her father. It was too much fun to play with them. To enjoy the company of a man for a night or two and then move on to someone else.

Leaving the man she'd been with wanting more.

Something about Colton got under her skin though. Odd, seeing as though they'd just met. Maybe it was the rumble of his laughter or the smoldering way he looked at her. The easy confidence in his stride. He looked like he wasn't used to taking no for an answer, but she also had the feeling that if she bowed out now, he'd let her go.

Regretfully, perhaps.

But he wasn't the type of man to force a woman into something she didn't want to do.

He was as opposite from her father and his men as one could be.

"Wait here, kitten," he said, setting her suitcase down and easing their bags off his shoulder and onto the ground near the seating area. "I need to go check in." His hand slid over her sleek suitcase, and he patted it once. "This looks expensive."

"I have expensive tastes. But not to worry, my taste in men has never been wrong."

Colton's eyes heated as he looked at her. "My taste in women has always been impeccable as well." He ducked lower, his lips brushing against her ear, sending shivers racing through her body. She stilled as his hand wrapped around her upper arm, the slow movement of his thumb caressing her skin making her wish he'd touch her everywhere. "And I plan on tasting every part of you, kitten," he said, his voice thick with promise. "Be right back."

He released her, leaving her momentarily stunned as he crossed the lobby to the front desk.

Maybe a man like him was more dangerous than she thought.

Camila watched him walk toward the desk, his jeans hanging just so from his narrow hips. Her eyes ran up his body, over his strong back and broad shoulders. Two women standing off to the side whispered about him, and she smirked as they glanced back at her.

Sitting down on one of the plush chairs in the lobby, she reached into her tote bag and pulled out her small mirror and red lipstick. Carefully reapplying it, she smacked her lips together as a shadow suddenly fell over her.

Her gaze swept up to Colton. "All set, kitten," he said, the corner of his mouth quirking up. "I even arranged to have room service arrive in ten minutes."

"*Perfecto*," she said, allowing Colton to take her hand as she stood. "*Adoro champan.*"

His eyebrows raised.

"I adore champagne," she said with a laugh.

He chuckled, his large, warm hand wrapping around hers as he tugged her closer. Shivers raced down her spine at his touch, and she gazed up at him, her eyes falling on his full lips. People milled around about them, but Colton ducked down, his mouth softly landing on hers.

She moved closer, pulling her hand free from his to run her fingers up his muscular chest. He groaned as he kissed her again, more deeply, and then stepped back.

She reached up and lightly brushed her lipstick off

his mouth, enjoying the feel of his warm lips beneath his fingers. The scruff of his jaw against her hand. Reluctantly, she pulled away.

"Let's get to our room, kitten. We've got all night," he said, his voice husky.

"That we do," she agreed, her body alight at his touch. Even with that one simple kiss, arousal had coiled low in her belly, snaking down lower still until she throbbed for his touch. Her nipples pebbled against her lace bra, and her thoughts whirled.

Colton grabbed their bags, and she imagined those large, muscular hands dragging all over her entire body. Those thick arms caging her in as he prowled over her on the bed, ready to thrust deep inside her welcoming body.

Holy hell.

The man had barely even touched her.

She smiled coyly at him in the elevator, her gaze trailing down his body until it landed at the bulge in his pants.

The very *large* bulge.

He was all brawn and muscle and had the goods to go with it. Yum.

The number twelve lit up after a few moments, and they stepped off the elevator together. Colton gestured for her to go ahead, and she confidently strode down the hallway, unable to resist slightly swaying her hips as she walked.

She felt his heated gaze on her almost as if it were a caress. A smile played at her lips.

"Last door on the right, kitten. We're room 1200."

She glanced back over her shoulder, tousling her hair and pouting her lips as she did. Not that she needed to get Colton's attention. His heated eyes were already on her as he practically swaggered down the hallway after her.

The ornate decorations of the luxury hotel—gorgeous wallpaper, crystal light fixtures, and immaculately framed mirrors—stood in stark contrast to his rugged masculinity. Colton's broad shoulders and muscular arms almost looked as if they wouldn't even fit through a doorway. It was hard to believe any room could contain a man with as much leashed strength as him.

Even moving down the hallway after her, an energy sizzled around him. He was too big, his personality too strong to be contained by these walls. And all that energy and focus was about to be unleashed on her.

A beat later, and he was behind her at the door to their room, caging her in. His thick erection ground against her backside as he pressed against her, the heat and strength of his body causing a thrill to shoot straight though her. He ducked lower and whispered into her ear as he slid the keycard into the door. His hand lightly caressed her hip, and then the door was finally opening, Colton hot on her heels.

Their bags landed in a jumbled heap on the floor, and Colton's hands gripped her waist as she turned toward him, his mouth hot on hers as she wrapped her arms around his neck. Holy mother of God. The man was large everywhere. Her breasts rubbed against his solid chest, her flat stomach against his rock-hard erection. He lifted her easily into his arms, and she wrapped her legs around his waist, letting her espadrille sandals fall to the floor.

His palms came to her ass, and then he was rubbing her up and down his hard length. She whimpered against him—actually *whimpered* for this man. Even through their layers of clothing she could feel him nudging against her exactly where she needed it.

Exactly where she wanted him.

"Camila," he breathed.

"Take me to bed," she commanded.

Colton's eyes heated, and he walked over to the massive king-sized bed as he held her, every step jostling her against him even more. He didn't bother with any pretenses, just lay her down on the plush bedspread, his hands landing on either side of her head as his body hovered above hers.

She didn't dare to move in that moment—taking in his heat, his powerful body above hers, his scent. Colton smelled of something slightly spicy and pure male. He stood, towering above her for a beat, his gaze roaming appreciatively over every inch of her body, like she was a feast he couldn't wait to devour. She enjoyed his eyes on her, the bulge in his pants. Most men were unable to resist her feminine curves. Her full breasts and rounded hips may have given her grief when she was younger, but as a woman?

She could have men practically eating out of her hands.

He stepped between her legs, and she trembled in anticipation. By now most men would be ripping her clothes off in eagerness.

Biting, pawing, pulling their erection free.

But Colton?

His fingers lightly ran up her bare legs, the soft touch teasing her more than any roughness would. He watched his hands moving over her skin, seeming entranced at the differences between them. The bulges of the tendons on his hands stood out in harsh contrast to her smooth skin. He was big and rough and strong and somehow also impossibly gentle with her.

She whimpered as his hands skimmed across her inner thighs, her panties damp with arousal. He hadn't even undressed her yet, and her clit throbbed for his touch, her nipples taut against the top of her outfit.

Colton paused only as he reached the shorts of her trendy romper, his fingers lightly sliding under the material. "Hell. I forgot this wasn't a dress," he said, his eyes narrowing.

Camila laughed, momentarily regaining control. He'd barely been touching her, but she'd been completely entranced by him. Held in place on the bed by only his look. By the chemistry surging between them—some invisible string that had seemed to tether them together. "No problem, lover," she said, sitting up as Colton stepped back. "Help me undress?"

Colton's hands were on her in an instant as he helped her to stand. Skimming over her clothing. Caressing her skin. "My pleasure," he said, his voice deep. His eyes heated with arousal. "Those might've been the sexiest damn words I've ever heard you utter."

"You barely even know me—"

She gasped as he ducked down and kissed her neck, his teeth grazing against her tender skin, his fingers running through her long hair. He nipped at her again, causing her to arch up and thrust her breasts against him. He growled in approval, his rough hands moving lower and pulling the straps off her shoulders. His gaze fell to her full breasts, now rapidly rising and falling, and then he was ducking lower and kissing her cleavage.

Leaving her whimpering before him.

"God you're gorgeous," he murmured a moment later as he slid the top further down, revealing her lace-clad breasts. His hands paused at her waist, and she chuckled as she realized why he'd suddenly stopped.

"You have to unzip the side. A woman has hips, no?"

"Hell, who came up with this? Take it off before I tear the damn thing in half."

"My, my, such a temper," she teased, playfully putting her hand in the middle of his chest and lightly pushing him back.

Colton took one step backward and then stood perfectly still, barely daring to move, and she saw his Adam's apple bob as he swallowed. She turned to the side, enjoying the affect she was having on him. Glancing at Colton over her shoulder, and slowly unzipped the side of her romper, playfully showing him the edge of her red lace thong.

"Hell. And now you're stripping for me," he said, his voice gravel. He practically shook as he stood in place, ready to move toward her again, and she admonished him. He fisted his hands at his sides as she smiled.

"Tsk, tsk. You have to wait until I undress. You only get to look before you touch."

He growled as she pushed her outfit down her legs, shimmying to get it all the way off. She stepped out of it and turned in a full circle, clad only in her red lacy bra and thong. Time seemed to stand still as she once again stood facing him, and then suddenly he was moving forward. Sweeping her up into his arms.

He lay her down on the bed and prowled on top of her, holding himself up with his muscular arms. "You're such a tease, kitten. But two can play at that game."

"Oh?" she asked, biting her lip as she looked at him in challenge.

"Oh yes," he said gruffly, moving one large hand to her breast, letting his fingers trace over the red lace cup. She whimpered as the fabric rubbed against her peaked nipple, and then he palmed her entire breast, capturing her cries with a kiss.

Warm lips moved against hers, and then his tongue was demanding entrance. Sliding against hers. Claiming her mouth.

He kneaded her breast before grazing his thumb over her nipple, sending her into a new frenzy of desire. Arousal dampened her thong panties, and Colton nudged her legs apart with one of his own. He kissed his way down her body, his hands and mouth everywhere. Her breasts spilled over the top of her bra as he tugged the cups down, and then he was kissing, suckling her. Teasing each nipple into a hardened tip.

A few swipes of his tongue had her crying out. Clutching the bedspread with her hands.

He kissed his way lower, across her flat stomach. Her fingernails raked against his head, her red polish a sharp contrast to his dark hair. Was she urging him on or begging him to stop? But then he was moving lower. He hovered above her pussy for a moment before completely passing it over while she groaned in frustration.

"Do you need me, kitten?" he asked huskily, slowly moving his mouth up one inner thigh. His light kisses and nips had her shaking as he approached her sex. His knuckles lightly brushed over her mound, and then he moved to her other leg, kissing and nibbling her other thigh as she helplessly bucked up against nothing.

"Kiss me," she demanded.

She felt his breath against her leg as he chuckled. "I am kissing you, kitten. I plan to kiss your entire body. I want my mouth over every single inch of your skin."

She mumbled in Spanish, knowing he wouldn't understand a single word she was saying, and then whimpered as he finally worked his way toward her sex again. He hovered above her pussy, exactly where she needed him.

"Do you have any more of these?" he asked, his voice dark. His thick fingers ran under the edge of her thong.

"*Sí*. An entire drawerful at home."

"Then you won't miss this one," he said, ripping it right off her. She gasped in surprise, but then he was pushing her legs farther apart. Kissing her swollen folds as he settled her legs over his broad shoulders. Spreading her wide for his taking.

"I'm in charge now, kitten," he said, using his thumbs to part her lower lips and grant him further access to her.

"Colton," she gasped, for once at a complete loss for words. She murmured in Spanish as he began to pleasure her. He teased and lapped at her pussy, tracing his tongue through every fold as she writhed on the bed.

She cried out, trying to buck against him, and his hands gripped her hips in an iron hold.

She was completely bared to him, vulnerable with her legs spread over his broad shoulders, and Colton hadn't even undressed yet.

Moving lower, he gently penetrated her core, thrusting his tongue in and out, and she lightly bucked up against him, helpless to his demands. Two thick fingers replaced his tongue as he began licking her sex again, and she cried out as he finally circled her swollen clit.

He began to thrust his fingers in and out as her inner walls tightened around him, and then he sucked her swollen bud into his mouth, teasing her mercilessly with his tongue. She gasped for breath, crying out as he built her up, and then just as she was about to fall over the edge, he pulled back, leaving her practically sobbing.

He kissed her thigh softly as her inner walls clamped down around nothing, her body aching to be filled. Consumed. Claimed by this man. She panted for breath and cursed at him in Spanish, desperate for release.

Colton chuckled, enjoying this far too much. "I told you I was going to tease you, kitten."

"You fight dirty!"

"Hell. I could go down on you all night. I could spend hours—days—lapping up your arousal. Making you fall apart from only my mouth."

He moved closer and kissed her core again as sparks of arousal shot straight through her. Her nipples hardened into aching peaks, her clit throbbed, and she lay gasping, spread wide before Colton as he did whatever he pleased.

"What do you need, kitten? Just tell me."

"Colton!"

He slowly moved his tongue over her folds again as her breasts rose up and down, lazily lapping up her arousal as he purposefully avoided her clit. His tongue found her slick channel once more, and he slowly thrust it inside, moving way too slowly to grant her any form of release.

To give her anything near what she needed.

She cried out again, moving against him as he pulled back. "Tell me, kitten," he said, kissing her sex again before hovering above it. "Tell me what you need."

"Please," she said, bucking up toward him.

"Please what?" he hinted, a smug look on his chiseled features.

Her legs shook on top of his shoulders, and she whimpered as his lips barely brushed against her quivering folds. He lightly kissed her again, the barest hint of a touch.

"Colton," she begged, "please make me come!" She tossed her head back and forth, her hands fisting the bedspread as Colton finally obliged and lightly flicked her clit with his tongue. She cried out, the touch nearly too much to bear.

Colton eased two, then three thick fingers inside her, thrusting them in and out of her hot, slickened channel. Arousal dampened her thighs she was so wet and ready for him.

And then he sucked on her clit. Hard.

She screamed, helplessly bucking against his face as she exploded, her orgasm going on and on. She tried to pull away as the sensations finally became too much, but he gripped one of her hips, holding her to him. Determined to wring every last ounce of pleasure out of her.

She cried out his name as he somehow brought her to orgasm again, Colton feasting on her pussy as her legs remained splayed over his shoulders, her body his to command. She bucked and writhed as her sex fluttered against his mouth, her orgasm going on and on.

Breathless, she finally collapsed on the bed, utterly spent.

Colton eased his fingers from her and softly kissed her sex, letting her down from her climax. Her legs trembled as he slid them from his shoulders, and her chest heaved up and down.

"Hell, kitten," he said, licking her arousal from his fingers before prowling back up her body, his muscular frame caging her in. His hardened cock pressed against her, still constrained in his jeans. "You're the sweetest damn thing I ever tasted."

"Colt—oh my God," she gasped.

"Shh," he said, tugging her bra back into place and pulling the covers around her. Her red lacy thong lay flung on the floor beside her red outfit. "Sleep."

She gazed at him in an orgasm-induced haze, and briefly closed her eyes as he ducked down to kiss her temple.

A moment later, she was fast asleep.

Chapter 3

Colton emerged from the bathroom the next morning, his gaze landing on Camila sleeping on the king-sized bed, her gorgeous body only partially hidden by the tousled sheets. Her smooth caramel skin contrasted with the white cotton, her breasts barely covered by the white fabric, the sumptuous globes looking ripe and tempting. Her tousled dark hair fell softly around her shoulders, and one shapely leg came out from where the sheet was loosely wrapped around her.

And she was stunning.

Gorgeous.

The type of woman he could get used to waking up next to, if he believed in that sort of thing.

The early morning Miami sun peeked in through the curtains, and he crossed the hotel room, pulling them fully shut.

Biding himself a little more time alone with her.

He strode back over toward Camila, his erection

straining against his boxer briefs. He wasn't above waking her up for a quick romp between the sheets, but she looked so goddamned peaceful and innocent at the moment.

Camila innocent, he thought with a smirk.

She was more like a seductress, determined to wring every last ounce of pleasure out of him.

But the soft way her hair fell across her face, her body relaxed in slumber made him see her in an entirely different way.

Rather than her tempting and teasing him, enjoying the ways she could give him pleasure, she looked fragile. Feminine in her beauty, but in a way that brought forth his protective instincts. Sure, last night he'd happily stripped her clothes right off of her and taken her again and again, enjoying how she'd cried out his name.

But now?

He wanted to wrap her up and keep her safe.

Not send her on the next flight to Bogota.

Not give her right back to her father.

He glanced at his phone, noting the text message lighting up the screen saying that his flight had been rescheduled for later this morning. No surprise given the bright sunshine outside. The storm had moved on overnight, just like he would in a couple hours.

The slight pang of regret in his chest was something he didn't want to examine too closely.

Camila stirred, rustling lightly beneath the twisted sheets as he set his phone back on the nightstand. Her eyes opened, watching him sleepily.

"Good morning, kitten."

His voice was husky. Soft. Not demanding like it had been last night, when he'd enjoyed pleasuring her in every way imaginable.

Her gaze drifted over his bare chest and fell to his erection. "A very happy morning, indeed."

Colton smirked, the bed sinking as he sat down beside her. As she watched him with hooded eyes, he was unable to resist running a hand down her bare arm.

Her skin was so impossibly soft and smooth.

"We could order room service," he said, his voice low.

"Why waste our time on food?" she asked, turning so the sheet fell lower across her. She sat up, loosely holding the sheet to her stomach, her full breasts in glorious display. Large nipples stood out against her caramel skin, and he resisted the urge to touch. Taste.

Claim what was his once more.

Cocking her head slightly, she smiled. "Cat got your tongue? I mean certainly you've seen a naked woman before, no? A woman aside from me?"

Colton chuckled, his gaze dancing over her bare flesh. He met her playful gaze. "I need to keep up my strength. You brought me to my knees last night, kitten."

Camila laughed, that rich throaty sound he loved so much. His eyes were drawn downward once more, to her full breasts bouncing lightly up and down. Hell, he could watch her all day long.

Forever.

"All right," she agreed. "Room service then."

"Then what?" he asked huskily, watching as she reached across him for the menu, completely uninhibited. Such a change from some of the women he usually spent the night with—the type who didn't want to be seen without makeup on and every hair perfectly in place.

Maybe Camila was still wearing makeup from last night—how the hell would he know. But she wasn't rushing to the bathroom to quick touch up everything. He'd mostly noticed her red lipstick last night, and that had quickly disappeared after a night of lovemaking.

Lovemaking. Shit.

He'd taken her to bed for a one-night-stand. Distracted her so he could bug her belongings and track down her father.

When the hell had he become so damn sappy?

"Mmm," she said, her red manicured nail running down the menu. "I'll just have fruit and toast. And coffee of course."

"Of course," he murmured, glancing at the menu himself.

"Why don't you order while I go freshen up?" she asked, letting the sheet drop completely as she stood. He watched as she walked toward the bathroom fully nude, her shapely calves and legs leading up to her gorgeous rounded ass. Her hair moved around her slender shoulders as she walked, and she turned to blow him a kiss before walking into the bathroom. His cock hardened at the sight of her bare breasts. And then she disappeared, pulling the door shut behind her.

He muttered a curse as he heard the shower starting.

Room service could wait if it meant he'd get to see Camila, dripping wet. If it meant his hands could be running all over her gorgeous body. If his cock could be thrusting into her tight pussy.

He stripped off his boxer briefs and crossed the

room, enjoying the way she squealed in delight as he joined her in the shower.

***

"Making a call?" she asked thirty minutes later, emerging from the bathroom clad in only a large white bath towel.

Colton tucked his phone in his cargo pants, his eyes shielded from her. "Yep. Just had to check in with the boss. The flight delay changed my plans and all."

She watched him for a moment before padding across the room. "Ugh. I'm dreading returning to reality," she said, flopping down onto the bed. "Give me another few days in Miami, and I'll be a happy woman."

A knock sounded at the door, and Colton crossed the room to get their room service cart. He glanced back at her, and she smiled and stepped out of view from the door. "You're for my eyes only, kitten," he said, his voice husky.

"Meow," she teased, and he chuckled.

Something about the possessiveness in his voice thrilled her. As did the smoldering look he gave her when he brought their food into the room.

"Everything all right?" he asked a moment later, noticing the frown on her face as he poured them two cups of coffee and uncovered the plates. She tossed her phone onto the bed and picked up one of the cups, taking a small sip of the delicious dark roast.

"It will be—just family stuff. My father wasn't too happy I spent an additional night in Miami as it is. He prefers having me close by, where he knows exactly what I'm doing at all times."

"Your father?" Colton asked, taking a bite of the four-egg omelet he'd ordered. Complete with ham, cheese, and a dizzying amount of vegetables. Compared to her own small bowl of fruit and slices of toast, he'd ordered enough food to feed an army. She wondered again what he did—not that they'd had much time for small talk.

Something physical, for certain.

He was pure muscle beneath that tanned, masculine flesh. Rock hard where she was soft. And his body moving confidently over hers had been a dream. The stuff fantasies were made of.

Colton was a wonder with his mouth and hands—and that magnificent cock of his. She'd been more than happy to play with him last night. And he'd certainly surprised her with the endless number of ways they'd made love. Camila had expected him to be ready for some quick and dirty sex, but the way he'd repeatedly sought her pleasure?

Made her beg and plead to come?

Heat rose within her just recalling it.

"My father loves to control my life," she said, a frown forming on her face. "Sure, he gives me plenty of money for shopping, traveling, dinners out, and the like, but as for doing anything else? *Nada.* He wants me under his control."

Colton cleared his throat, those observant eyes watching her. "He wants to control you? Has he hurt you?" he asked, his voice lowering even more. He sat impossibly still, his eyes trained on her.

Camila laughed, the humor not reaching her eyes. "My father thinks women are good as only two things—lovers or prostitutes. But no, he hasn't laid a finger on me. Nor will anyone else. When I'm in Colombia, I have bodyguards with me at all times. No freedom without him knowing where I go. No privacy since I have guards with me at all times. It's complicated."

Colton let out a low whistle. "Sounds like it. Why don't you leave?"

She shrugged. "It's not really an option. Where would I go? What would I do? I suppose he'd let me leave—as in, if I managed to come to the U.S. or somewhere, he wouldn't chase after me. But how would I live? He'd cancel all my credit cards. Close my accounts. It's not like I can just walk around with huge amounts of cash without anyone asking me questions. I could take some money and leave, but how far would I get? In every sense of the word, I'm trapped."

"I don't like it," Colton muttered, stabbing at his omelet.

"What's there to like?" she asked with a bitter laugh. "It doesn't concern you anyhow, so no need to worry. This is rather deep for a one-night-stand anyway."

His eyes met hers. "I'm worried about you."

"There's no need for you to worry. You'll go on with your life, and I'll go on with mine. Besides, a woman like me can take of herself."

She took another sip of her coffee, suddenly losing her appetite. It was foolish, perhaps. To want another life. Her father never let her want for anything—and that was possibly the entire problem. She had a social life and large allowance for her shopping sprees, for the travel he agreed to. She had men to guard her every movement. To chauffeur her around.

But freedom?
A choice as to how to live her own life?
She was a prisoner.

Chapter 4

Colton muttered under his breath as he ducked into Anchors a week later, dodging two young sailors who'd already had a few too many. He stepped out of their way as they stumbled along, pausing at the front of the popular bar along the Virginia Beach strand where many of his military buddies hung out. Since it wasn't too far from Little Creek, it was always filled with plenty of sailors, SEALs, and single women, and tonight didn't disappoint.

A group of giggling women whispered and gawked at him as they walked out the front door, their skimpy tank tops covering their string bikinis, and Colton resisted the urge to roll his eyes.

There was something to be said about the thrill of the chase.

Block after block of bikini-clad women lounging at the beach and walking down the boardwalk, visiting the numerous restaurants and bars dotting Virginia Beach, wasn't exactly a challenge. And drunk women falling all over him didn't exactly have quite the same appeal as getting the attention of a gorgeous yet confident and elusive woman.

A woman who knew she was a prize to be caught. Savored. Treasured.

Like Camila.

Legs for days, lush brown locks he didn't want to stop running his hands through, and curves dangerous enough to give a man a heart attack.

Memories of their night together would fucking haunt him for the rest of his life. It must've been the temptation of what he couldn't have. Because he'd spent plenty of nights with a woman in his bed over the years and never wanted to chase her down a week later.

There'd been lots of spectacular sex that he'd told his buddies about the next day.

But with her?

"Yo! C-4!" his buddy Mason hollered from the back of Anchors.

Colton's gaze swept to the table several of the men on his SEAL team occupied. Sitting alongside Mason were Noah "Viper" Miller, his aviators perched atop his head, and Jacob "Joker" Olson. Mason, one of the younger guys on the team, was laughing as he took their longnecks from the tray that the pretty waitress was carrying. Jacob was howling with laughter beside him, his date for the evening looking less than amused.

Noah nodded as he spotted Colton heading their way but stood and followed a group of women walking to a nearby table. Colton's gaze trailed after them as he watched Noah wrap his arms around two of the women.

He shook his head as he approached his buddies. Some things never changed.

"What's so damn funny?" Colton asked the rest of the group, pulling up a chair as their laughter began to die down.

"Not much," Jacob's girl said, pouting, as the other men continued to flirt with their waitress.

"Baby, don't be like that," Jacob said, putting his arm around her shoulders. She relaxed into him, clearly enjoying the attention, and Colton watched as Jacob's fingers grazed over her bare shoulder. Instantly his mind flashed back to a week ago Miami—

Undressing Camila in his hotel room. Sliding the straps of that sexy little sundress—romper—whatever the hell she called it—off of her smooth, creamy shoulders.

Kissing every inch of her skin. Parting her thighs as he ducked lower, inhaling her intoxicating scent as he went down on her.

Camila's red lips wrapped around his dick as she sucked him off later that night.

Fuck.

One week later, and he still couldn't get the gorgeous, exotic woman out of his mind. He wasn't normally the type of man to pine after a woman or want more than one night with her in his bed, but holy hell. What a woman she was.

It was all he could do to let her get on her flight to Colombia the next morning and not drag her back to the hotel room for a few more rounds between the sheets.

And in the shower.

Up against the dresser.

On the floor.

He'd bugged her belongings when she'd been sleeping—placing the GPS trackers he'd acquired on her fancy suitcase, tote bag, even putting a microscopic one on her lipstick. If it had been a planned op, they'd have better quality surveillance available to them.

As it was?

They'd been able to follow her every movement.

Giving them an excellent idea where her father and possibly other cartel members were.

It figured that the woman he'd become nearly infatuated with was literally the enemy. A woman he could enjoy one steamy, unforgettable night with but never see again.

"Can I get you a beer, too, Colt?" the waitress asked, holding the now-empty tray in one hand. Since the guys were regulars here, she knew them all by name. She blushed prettily as Mason said something else, and Colton raised his eyebrows in amusement.

"Don't worry about it," she said. "I managed."

"Hell sweetheart," Mason said. "If that happens again, you give me a call."

"What'd I miss?" Colton asked. "Something bad happened?"

"Taylor had car trouble, and some asshole ripped her off," Mason said. "Charged her $400 just for a tow."

Colton grimaced and let out a low whistle. He also didn't miss the fact that Mason was now on a first-name basis with her.

"Well, it's over and done with now," Taylor said lightly. "I'm perfectly capable of taking care of myself. So what about that beer?"

"Sure thing," Colton said, his eyes darting between her and Mason. Her cheeks were slightly flushed, and he didn't miss the way Mason couldn't keep the grin off his face as he watched her.

"Coming right up," Taylor said before turning and walking away. The guys watched her walk off before Jacob elbowed Mason in the ribs.

"You got a thing for her?" Jacob asked. "What makes you think she'd want your sorry ass?"

Mason clutched his hand to his heart, pretending to be wounded. "Ouch. Are you sure you want to hang out with this guy?" he asked Jacob's date. "There's lots of other available men around here," he joked.

"You're right. Maybe I should've picked another Navy SEAL from the Delta team," she teased. "Where's Ryker anyway?"

The other men at the table guffawed. Although all of the guys on their SEAL team enjoyed the company of a beautiful woman, Ryker "Bull's Eye" Fletcher was probably the biggest ladies' man of them all. He'd never been turned down by a woman he wanted to take home, thus the "Bull's Eye" moniker the other guys had given him.

If Ryker wanted a woman, he always hit his target.

And he wasn't even here at Anchors tonight.

"Hell. He's probably balls deep in a woman now," Jacob said with a grin. "You're gonna have to pick someone else or just settle for me."

Colton smirked as the woman at Jacob's side blushed, shushing him.

There seemed to always be a woman or two hanging out with their group when they went out for drinks. But although each of the guys enjoyed the company of a beautiful woman willing to go home with him at the end of the night, most were content to play the field. The women's faces changed, but their team nights at Anchors stayed the same.

And the guys on their team wouldn't have it any other way.

Aside from Ryker, the only other man missing tonight was Hunter. And he was probably off playing house with his new girlfriend—or getting laid.

Amazing how the thought of a woman in your bed every night was enough to make a guy give up his regular nights out. Hunter still came out with them some of the time, but damn.

That guy was pussy whipped. And loving every minute of it.

Noah sauntered back over a few minutes later, dragging an empty chair to the table and taking a seat.

"What happened to the women you were with?" Colton asked, raising his eyebrows. "They get tired of you already?"

"We're heading out in thirty," Noah said with a smirk, his piercing green eyes looking amused. "They needed some girl time to make plans. The hell if I know."

"And what makes you think we want you back here after ditching us for those babes?" Mason ribbed him.

"Don't worry, I talked you up to them, too," Noah said with grin.

"Hell yeah," Mason said, taking a pull of his beer as he gazed over at the group of women.

Noah smirked. "I figured you could use the help. After I pick the woman I want, I'll let you choose from the leftovers."

The rest of the table broke out in whoops and hollers.

Their waitress appeared just then, carrying a tray of wings and sliders. Colton nabbed his beer from the full tray, and she shot him a grateful look. "Thanks, sweetheart," Mason said with a wink. Colton didn't miss the slight hint of pink once again spreading over her cheeks.

"Just let me know if you boys need anything else."

"Just your phone number," Jacob said with a grin. "For Mason here, of course. I've already got a beautiful date tonight."

Taylor turned ten shades of red as Mason shot Jacob a look that could kill. "He's just teasing you, sweetheart. Not that I wouldn't love to take you out sometime."

"I don't date customers," she murmured hastily before turning and leaving.

Colton raised his eyebrows.

She was in such a rush to leave, she hadn't even asked if they needed anything else.

"Blown off," Mason said with a chuckle. "Maybe I can sweet talk her into a date another night."

"All right, we're heading out," Jacob said, taking a final pull of his beer before pushing his chair back and standing up with his date. He snaked his arm around her waist, pulling her close. "We've got some quality time to spend together, right baby?"

The rest of the team said their goodbyes, and then Colton was left alone with Mason and Noah.

"Think we'll get called up this weekend?" Mason asked.

"Tough to say," Colton said. "The CO seemed to think the deployment is imminent. Just waiting on word from the Pentagon."

During their briefing that morning, Delta's CO had updated them on the pending op. The team was planning to move in and snatch an infamous drug lord in Bogota after the intel was final. And not just the head of any cartel— Miguel Rodriguez.

Camila's father.

Ironic that she'd been reluctant to give him her last name when he'd known who she was all along. She'd been his target from the moment he stepped foot in Miami International Airport.

The fact that he'd ended up taking her to bed was just a bonus. He'd had plenty of one-night-stands during his career in the Navy. Women he'd meet at a bar, take home for the night, and then never see again. He'd never been with a woman that he'd set out intentionally to find though. One that he'd needed something from.

Getting her into bed had been damn near too easy. Unnecessary, too, since he'd bugged her suitcase right in the lobby of the hotel. He could've been on his way, never to see her again. Going through her belongings after making love to her had gotten additional information for the Pentagon though.

And the fact that she'd turned out to be a sex kitten?

That he now couldn't get her out of his mind?

Colton took a long pull of his beer.

He'd didn't feel an ounce of regret at sleeping with her. But the fact that he wouldn't see her again? Something about that left him uneasy.

"Hell. Is Alpha coming with us?" Noah asked. The Alpha and Delta SEAL teams were both based out of Little Creek and had worked together recently rescuing an American woman being held hostage in the Middle East. The op had gone FUBAR though, with the Alpha team leader Patrick "Ice" Foster getting injured and medevac'd to Landstuhl.

The woman had been successfully rescued though, and everyone eventually made it back to the States in one piece.

"I don't know if Alpha is coming on this one," Colton said. "They were originally supposed to be lead, but it sounds like they're needed elsewhere. Ice should be back."

"I thought he was back on active duty a while ago," Mason said.

"He went on his damned honeymoon," Noah guffawed. "Hell, you'll never see me falling into that trap."

"Trap?" Colton asked, chuckling. "I'll admit I don't particularly want to get married at the moment, but I'm not sure if 'trap' is the word I'd use."

"Not if you want to get laid again," Mason said with a smirk. "Better to act like you're not completely opposed to marriage. Not that I'm in a rush to ever settle down. There's too many single and available women out there."

"Amen to that," Noah said, tipping his beer toward them before downing a couple of sliders.

Colton took a pull of his beer, unease settling in his gut as Mason and Noah continued to talk about the pending mission. It was likely the Delta team would be deployed to South America within the next week. Possibly even straight to Colombia if Camila's dad was still there.

Hell.

He didn't like the idea of running a mission where

she could potentially be in harm's way. Yes, she was the daughter of a notorious drug lord, but she didn't seem privy to any of the operations from what he could garner. He'd gone through all of her belongings and cell phone when she'd been sound asleep.

After he'd made her come so many times throughout the night that he could've taken all her things and left if he'd wanted.

That's how sated and exhausted she'd been.

Not even so much as her father's name appeared anywhere. Not a hint that she knew anything about his drug running and sex trafficking ring. Colton had been able to copy her contact list and emails for the Department of Defense to examine, but damn.

The woman seemed clean.

And he had a gut instinct that she wasn't involved.

Noah stood a few minutes later, heading off with two of the women he'd met. Mason chuckled as they walked away. "Viper's thinking with his dick again."

Colton eyed the three of them moving toward the door. "No surprise there," he said, taking another pull of his beer.

"You planning on taking anyone home tonight?" Mason asked.

"Nah. Not in the mood for a clingy one-night-stand."

Camila's image flashed through his mind.

She'd flown back to Colombia with no idea who he was or that he was coming down there. She had no clue that he'd known exactly who she was from the moment they met. You couldn't make this shit up if you wanted to.

Chapter 5

Camila ducked into the café on the corner of the crowded street in Bogota, her vibrant sundress swishing around her as she wove her way between tables to get to her friend in the back. The top of the dress hugged her breasts, and a few men glanced up from their own table, eyeing her appreciatively.

"You made it," her friend Rosa said, tossing her blonde streaked hair over her shoulder. "I was beginning to think you wouldn't be able to come."

Camila dropped her shopping bags onto the tile floor, clutching her designer purse as she sat down in one of the chairs and crossed her legs. Expensive sandals showed off her new pedicure, and the men seated a few tables away glanced at her again, eyeing her toned legs.

"Barely," Camila said. "My meeting ran longer than I expected."

"Meeting?" Rosa asked with a laugh. "Looks like shopping." She took a sip of her coffee, blowing on it

49

as steam rose from the top.

"A little of this, a little of that," Camila said. "And then I had to wait until someone could escort me here," she said, tilting her head toward the windows at the front of the café. Her eyes settled on two of her father's men, standing outside. Tattoos wound their way up their muscled arms, and it was no secret they were carrying firepower. Each stood there threateningly, scanning the busy street as if it were the most natural thing in the world to hover outside of a café armed to the teeth.

Rosa raised her eyebrows. "You need two bodyguards now?"

Camila shrugged. "According to my father, yes. According to me, no. I'll try to see if I can lose them later. Nothing like trying to browse around and shop with two brutes on my tail."

Rosa laughed. "I'm sure they didn't mind admiring your backside."

Camila threw her arms in the air, rapidly muttering in Spanish. "My father pays them to watch out for trouble—not to be ogling me."

"I'm just saying," Rosa, said, taking another sip of her coffee. "They were watching you quite intently when you walked inside here a few minutes ago."

Camila resisted the urge to shudder. "Men always want what they cannot have, no? My father is more concerned about his rivals than them. Those two have been with him for years."

Rosa eyed her knowingly. "Be careful, Camila. With all the threats going on lately...." Her voice dropped to a whisper. "You know those other cartels want your father gone. Even men within the Rodriguez cartel itself want to take him out. He's been in power far too long for other men to not crave what he has."

Camila brushed her long, dark hair back over one shoulder. "I can take care of myself. Always have, always will. I refuse to rely on a man for anything—including my own father."

Rosa's eyes narrowed. "This isn't a joke. Maybe you could turn down a rich man at a nightclub, but a member of another cartel? A group of men after you? It's better those bodyguards are with you at all times. Whether you like it or not."

Camila pressed her lips together. Her brief escape to Miami a week ago had been wonderful—literally a breath of fresh air. No need to watch her back every moment. The freedom to come and go where she chose. She didn't have to be escorted by armed men everywhere she went.

And then there was the extra night she stayed.

Colton.

She'd teased and taunted him for sure.

But he'd met her move for move. Kissing and caressing every inch of her skin until she was writhing on the bed, literally begging him for more.

A waitress walked over to their table, and Camila's thoughts were instantly back in the café. On her friend. Her eyes darted again to the men outside, now conferring intently with one another. She ordered a coffee and eyed Rosa as their waitress walked away. "It's been this way for a while now. The rival cartels looking to take over the market. The new members wanting to unseat my father from his position of power." She shrugged. "My father always comes out ahead. Everyone knows this."

Rosa shook her head. "If your father's own men

turn against him? That's not anything you can stop."

"Pffft. Too many of the men have been with him for years. They're seduced by the allure of money and power and women. Why would they go against him?"

"Because they want it ALL. Not just whatever Miguel Rodriguez is willing to hand out to them. Besides. Three more women have gone missing." She raised her eyebrows, pointedly eyeing Camila.

Everyone in Bogota knew why the women had vanished. Maybe they didn't know the specific location, the specific men who had taken them. But the why? The how?

The Rodriguez cartel had been kidnapping more women left and right. The entire city was afraid—and rightfully so. Camila and Rosa might be safe, but other women their age?

"You know I don't have a say in my father's operations. I don't think it's right either, to kidnap and sell innocent women. But what am I supposed to do? Even the police won't do anything to find them. My father has them under his thumb even more than his own men."

"Money talks," Rosa said, rubbing her thumb and fingers together.

Camila laughed. "I have money, sure. But my father pays them far more than I ever could. And if he found out I went against him? That I did something to impede his entire operation? He'd sell me off to the highest bidder."

Rosa snorted. "He wouldn't. His only daughter? If anything, he loves taunting his men with you too much."

Camila's eyes narrowed. "That would be infinitely worse. A rich man paying for a woman would be preferable in about a thousand ways to letting those thugs have their way with me."

The waitress nearly dropped the tray, clumsily setting Camila's coffee down in front of her. Some of the dark black brew sloshed over the side of the mug. The waitress mumbled an apology, hastily dabbing it with some napkins before placing a small pitcher of creamer and a bowl of sugar cubes on the table.

She hurried back toward the kitchen before even asking if they needed anything else.

Rosa glanced back at Camila. "I guess she overheard our conversation."

"It's no secret who I am."

Camila eyed her friend until she shrugged and changed the subject. "You never finished telling me about your trip to Miami last weekend. The other night you barely even looked at another man when we went out dancing. You? Camila Rodriguez? Not go home with a handsome stranger?" She laughed, and Camila couldn't hold back the smile playing at her lips.

"Did you meet someone there? You did!" she shrieked when Camila didn't immediately answer.

"I did meet a man. When I got stranded at Miami International Airport for the night?" She leaned forward in her seat. "Let's just say I wasn't alone. I had some *very* good company for the evening."

"Spill!" Rosa said, her eyes lighting up. "Is he American? Colombian? Incredibly handsome?"

Camila nodded, slowly stirring sugar and creamer into her coffee. "*Si.* American. Very handsome. And very good in bed," she added with a throaty laugh.

Rosa smirked. "So, are you going to see him again? Maybe another impromptu trip to Miami is in order?"

"I won't see him again. We spent the night together but didn't exchange any contact information. I got on my flight to Colombia the next morning, and he headed off toward domestic departures. I can't even remember where he said he was going— somewhere in the States."

Rosa smiled knowingly. "Mmm-hmm. Not much time for chit-chat?"

Camila laughed. "We talked. Although mostly it was about all the ways he wanted me to scream his name."

Her friend giggled as she took a sip of her coffee. "So, he's a fantastic lover, and you didn't bother to get his name? What if he had a handsome brother for me to meet?"

"Oh, I got his name. Colton something or other." She shrugged.

"Are you blushing?" Rosa shrieked. "Camila Rodriguez blushing over a man?"

Camila tried not to laugh, a feeling of warmth washing over her. She smoothed her dress over her legs, remembering Colton's hands running over her thighs. "I may have cried out his name a few times in bed. He was very, very persuasive," she added with a wink. "But don't worry, my friend. He was shocked when I pleasured him, too. After all, I couldn't let him have all the fun."

"I don't doubt it. Word has gotten around about your expertise."

Camila pouted. "A gentleman never kisses and tells."

Rosa raised her eyebrows. "And who's to say the men you've been taking home with you are gentlemen?"

"Touché."

"What did you buy?" Rosa asked, eyeing the shopping bags on the floor. "Hopefully something in my size."

"A little of everything—new stilettos, a sexy little dress for the next time we go dancing. Perfume. Lingerie."

"What didn't you buy?" Rosa joked.

Camila waved her hand in a gesture of dismissal. "I needed something to do. My father wanted me out of the mansion for some important meeting he had. I'm not sure if he didn't want me to see what was going on or if he didn't want the men he was having over to see me."

"I'm worried about you."

"Me? Why?"

"You're completely oblivious to what's going on all around us."

Camila's gaze hardened. "Oblivious? No. I know what I can and can't do in my life. I'm lucky, yes—my father gives me everything. Money. Protection. A certain amount of power being that I'm his daughter. But I'm in a gilded cage, no? I can have what I want as long as I stay here and do exactly what he says."

Rosa nodded. "But are you happy living that way forever? You have fun seeing different men now, sure. But if you want your own family someday? If you ever fall in love?"

"Am I happy?" Camila asked in disbelief. "No. But what choices do I have?" She reached over and grabbed her purse, carefully pulling out her compact and reapplying her red lipstick.

"Exactly," Rosa chided. "You put on a happy face, looking the part, but inside? You'll never have what you really want."

Camila pursed her lips together, the truth of Rosa's words settling inside her. Her gaze shifted toward the door of the café as the two guards she was with suddenly came storming in. Camila watched, startled, as the biggest one moved to grab her arm. "We have to leave," he said, his voice gruff as his thick fingers wound around her bicep.

"Now? Why?" she asked, glancing around in confusion. There didn't appear to be any threats, either in the café or outside it. "We haven't even finished our coffee yet."

His grip on her arm tightened, and she winced in surprise. "Now," he repeated.

Her other bodyguard stood eyeing Rosa, his interest piquing. Camila's heart thumped in her chest, and she glanced from her friend toward the front door as she stood up. The other patrons in the café were beginning to take notice of their loud discussion, but none appeared interested in confronting her or her bodyguards.

She stumbled slightly in her high heeled sandals as the guard tugged her toward him.

"My bags," Camila said, reaching out as the first guard steered her away, bodily moving her toward the door.

"They stay," he said, his voice steel.

"Rosa," Camila said helplessly as the second bodyguard followed, the two men ushering her between the tables toward the front door. The other customers looked down, and their waitresses stood perfectly still, not daring to move.

Camila's purse lay on the table where she'd left it, her bags on the floor. Rosa looked slightly alarmed.

For the first time, Camila's chest tightened in panic. Her bodyguards weren't moving her out of the café for her protection. Weren't letting her gather up her things.

They were taking her. Hustling her toward a van idling on the street. Kidnapping her just like all the other women and girls who'd gone missing. Camila opened her mouth, ready to scream, when a dark cloth covered her face.

A sickeningly sweet smell overwhelmed her senses, and her mind began to fog. She fought to maintain her balance as she stumbled on the sidewalk, her dress blowing lightly in the wind.

Vice-like arms gripped her from behind, binding her arms to her sides, constricting her movement. She was too scared to scream. Too weak to fight back.

A man bodily lifted her into the waiting van.

And then everything faded to black.

Chapter 6

Colton scrubbed a hand across his day-old stubble, grabbing a chair in the bull-pen and sinking down into a seat. His rumpled shirt was tucked into his jeans, and the boots he'd pulled on in haste this morning weren't even tightened. The rest of his team shuffled around him, dragging chairs over as well for the impromptu 0500 meeting. They'd been called into base with less than an hour's notice, and Colton figured that whatever was happening was big.

Take-down a Colombian drug lord big.

Their team leader Hunter moved to the front of the room with Delta's CO, the two speaking in low voices as they conferred with one another while the massive flat-screen TV in front of them flickered with static, waiting for the secure connection to go through.

"You look like shit," Ryker said as he sat across from Colton, smirking. His gray eyes flickered with amusement.

Colton raised his eyebrows, glancing at his rumpled-looking teammate. "I didn't get all my beauty sleep last night. What'd you do? Roll out of bed and grab something from your dirty laundry?"

"Yeah, how'd you arrive looking fresh as a daisy?" Noah quipped sarcastically, his gaze landing on Ryker.

Ryker scowled as the other men on the team guffawed.

"Let me guess, you were otherwise occupied." Colton said. He crossed his arms and leaned back in the chair with a grin. "What'd you do? Sneak out on your one-night-stand?"

"No need to look so damn happy about it," Ryker muttered. "She was gorgeous. I had to leave her in bed and swing by my apartment to grab my ID to get onto base. Not exactly how I planned to start my morning."

"Hoorah," Noah said, adjusting the aviators atop his head with a smirk.

Their gazes all landed on the TV at the front of the room as the secure connection to the Pentagon finally went through. A moment later Admiral Pearson's face appeared on the screen, surrounded by a room full of military personnel and top brass at the Pentagon. "Good morning, team. By now you've received the latest SITREP on the situation in Colombia."

"Affirmative," their CO said. "I'll brief the Delta team on the latest updates. We can be ready to move out within the hour as soon as we receive orders, sir."

Colton raised his eyebrows. SITREPs, or situation reports, provided up-to-the minute intelligence on situations unfolding all over the world. The Delta team had been primed and ready to go for several days, waiting on word from the Pentagon as to when they'd make the move to deploy. An emergency briefing before going wheels up meant something else was going on.

A doorway behind him opened, and Colton glanced back to see Captain Ryan Mitchell, the Alpha SEAL team's CO, striding into the room. He nodded at the Delta team as he passed, his face stern and unreadable, before he stopped beside their own CO at the front.

"Captain Mitchell," the admiral addressed him. "What's the update on the situation in Kabul? Your team has moved out?"

He nodded. "Affirmative. The Alpha team went wheels up at 0400. They'll be ready to move in as soon as they land."

Admiral Pearson nodded and eyed the men on the Delta team from the secure video call. "As everyone is aware, the Alpha team was sent on another critical operation. They won't be deploying to Colombia with you. We've been waiting on intel for over a month to take down Miguel Rodriguez, the head of the Rodriguez cartel down in Bogota. Practically every damn three-letter agency has been involved gathering intelligence on this—DOD, DEA, FBI. Even the damn TSA is on alert at airports. We've had our eyes and ears open, and now is the chance to move in. Although we'd planned to send Alpha and Delta together, we don't have time to wait for their return. Rodriguez has been more accessible than usual due to the current situation unfolding. Now is our chance to bring him in."

"What situation is that, sir?" Hunter asked from beside the CO.

The admiral cleared his throat. "His daughter was kidnapped. The latest SITREP provides additional details, but it appears Rodriguez's own men have turned on him. The bodyguards of his own daughter nabbed her—possibly for their sex trafficking ring. Possibly for their own purposes. They could be demanding ransom. The intel is still out on the specifics. Rodriguez has been out in the open looking for answers, more careless about his security than ever before, and we're moving in to take him."

Colton blinked, momentarily in a daze at this new piece of information. Images from his night with Camila at the Miami hotel flashed through his mind. Her throaty laugh filled his ears. The memory of her scent slammed into him.

His gut clenched, and he ground his jaw, his blood boiling as he tried to focus on the secure feed. To listen to the rest of what the admiral was saying. His hands fisted at his sides, his anger a living, breathing thing.

"Camila?" he asked, his voice low.

As far as he knew Miguel Rodriguez only had one daughter.

But he needed to be certain. To make everything crystal clear.

His CO eyed him coolly, calmly assessing Colton's demeanor. "Affirmative."

All eyes swept back to Colton as he muttered a curse. "When?" His voice sounded hoarse. Desperate. Unlike him.

"Yesterday afternoon from a café in Bogota. Her bodyguards were right outside according to witness accounts, and then they rushed in and took her. Her friend was there, too, but left untouched. Nobody made any attempts to stop them. Not surprising, given that Miguel Rodriguez has even the local police under his control. She was thrown into a van and taken, location unknown at this time."

"Fuck," Colton muttered under his breath.

His CO addressed the admiral. "Colton put trackers on her belongings last week when he intercepted her at the airport. They could still lead us straight to Rodriguez if he's going after her himself."

"So, we're still able to track Camila?" Colton asked, something like hope springing forth in his chest. Adrenaline rushed through his veins, giving him purpose. Strength.

"Negative. She left everything in the café—purse, phone, belongings. Even if we wanted to flush out her father that way, we couldn't. It doesn't matter either way. Our operation isn't about recusing the woman—any of the women. We're taking down the kingpin."

Colton sat stiffly in his seat as the admiral continued the rest of the secure call, providing some details of the operation and other government agencies involved. And then just as quickly he dismissed them, turning off the feed to move on to other matters of national security with his team assembled at the Pentagon.

Some of the men began murmuring around him, and Colton's eyes landed on the CO.

"Is this personal?" his CO finally asked, eyeing him as static once again filled the screen behind him.

"Personal? No. Yes. Of course it's fucking personal," Colton spat out. "I spent the night with her at my hotel. In my hotel room."

Ryker snickered, and Colton shot him a look that

could kill.

"She was in my bed all goddamn night. And I went through her belongings—every last thing. She's clean. No trace of anything her father is involved in. You saw the emails we pulled. There's nothing that connects her to any of his operations."

"Then we move in and get her, too," Noah said. "Plus all those other innocent women who've been kidnapped."

"Not part of the op," their CO interjected. "If we find them along the way, we rescue them. Turn them over to the Colombian military. But we're not chasing after every damn woman they've nabbed. That would take weeks, months—hell, even years. Our mission is going in after one man."

Colton clenched his fists, resisting the urge to pound the table. To break something. To shout out in anger.

Hell.

He barely even knew the woman but knew he'd do anything in his power to rescue her. Protect her. Hell, he'd do everything. It wasn't even a question.

Ryker eyed him coolly from across the table, and Colton could practically see the wheels turning in his head. None of the team would abandon their mission, but when push came to shove, not one of the men was willing to leave a woman to be sold off as a sex slave.

And it wasn't just one woman.

There were hundreds who'd gone missing. The DOD didn't even know half of it.

"Get home and finish packing your gear," the CO said, glancing down at his phone. "We just got another SITREP. Attempts are being made to run

Rodriguez out of his mansion in Bogota. If he's hiding out, it will be harder to find him. We go wheels up at 0700. Less than two hours from now. Dismissed."

The men were on their feet in an instant, moving toward the door of the bullpen. And this was why Colton had never been in a serious relationship. Deploying on less than a couple of hours' notice didn't sit well with most women. Not when he couldn't tell them where he'd be going. How long he'd be gone.

Not when he'd up and leave at a moment's notice.

He walked out of base, the other men talking around him. Colton's gear had been packed and ready for imminent deployment. He'd grab a shower, gear up, and be back on base in less than an hour. Going to Colombia and leaving without Camila was not a goddamn option though.

Chapter 7

Camila's head pounded as she blinked and opened her eyes, the darkened room around her slowly coming into focus. Her mouth was dry and her stomach lurched as she tried to sit up from the mat she was lying on, her muscles stiff from the cramped position she'd been sleeping in. She fell back to the ground on her side, whimpering, but realized that she was unbound. Unharmed.

Aside from a slight ache in her upper arm from where her bodyguard had gripped her, she'd been left untouched.

For now.

She shuddered and hugged herself more tightly as her stomach roiled.

She felt too weak to do anything other than lie there, slowly breathing in and out. Slowly letting everything come back into focus. Hoping that the nausea would go away. What kind of chemical had been in that cloth they'd held over her face?

What else had they given her?

She recalled her bodyguards rushing into the café. Turning on her. She may not have been part of her father's operations, but everyone knew what he did.

Why they kidnapped women.

She clasped her legs tightly together, as if that would somehow prevent anyone from harming her. The silky sundress she was wearing had felt seductive and sexy before. Perfect for an afternoon of shopping and leisure. Maybe catching the eye of an attractive man as it swished around her legs as she moved.

Now she felt practically bare.

Exposed.

The thin material clung to her breasts, accented her shapely hips.

She gasped, panic rising within her. One of those animals could tear it right off her in an instant. And they wouldn't be gentle. They'd use and abuse her until there was nothing left.

She closed her eyes, blowing out a breath as her heart pounded and alternating waves of hot and cold washed over her. Was she having a panic attack? Responding to whatever they'd drugged her with?

A quiet cough from a few feet away had her opening her eyes once more. Blinking as she again took in the room.

Three other women lay on mats scattered around the floor, one in torn clothing. A purplish bruise was forming around her eye, and Camila's stomach lurched as the woman turned to the side and vomited. The smallest sliver of light was coming in through the lone window, a dark cloth tacked up over it. It was too high up and too small for any form of escape.

Not that Camila expected to be able to run freely if

she somehow did manage to get outside. Aside from the fact that she was clad only in her dress and heeled sandals, no doubt wherever they'd taken her was guarded.

And she was weak. Sick from whatever they'd drugged her with.

The concrete walls and floor and chill in the air made her think they were underground. Beneath a house or building perhaps. The cellar of a home or mansion.

Her own father's massive estate flashed through her mind. There were armed men constantly coming and going, forming a barrier of protection around the perimeter. None of that mattered now that her father's men had turned on him. On her. When her bodyguards had rushed into the café, she'd assumed they'd escort her out the back door. That it was unsafe out on the streets, or they saw someone they didn't like the look of.

Never in a million years did it occur to her that she'd be the one they were after—the biggest prize of them all.

Camila felt someone looking at her, her eyes settling on a young woman to her right. She had on jeans and a thin camisole, and her feet were bare. Dark circles under her eyes made her look even older than she probably was, and her hair was tangled and matted.

"Where are we?" Camila asked, her voice weak.

"Holding cell," the woman said, pushing herself up into a sitting position and leaning against the wall. She stretched her legs out in front of her, somehow managing to look unfazed by their current situation.

"A holding cell?"

"I've seen four women come and go," the woman said, coughing. "Today. Several others came and went yesterday. And the day before that. Nobody stays here for long."

Camila again tried to sit up, her body feeling like it was weighted down. Her arms wobbled, unsteady, her muscles refusing to hold her up. She collapsed back down to the mat in a huff of frustration.

"The drugs they gave you will wear off—until the next round. They barely give us any food or water down here, but what they do is laced with something. You'll be out for hours afterwards. They want us weak and complacent. Not much you can do unless you want to starve to death. Or die of thirst."

"How long have you been here?" Camila asked, her head spinning. Just that simple act of trying to sit up had left her reeling. If anyone were to come in here and take her?

She'd have no chance of fighting them off.

No hope of escape.

The woman shrugged. "A week maybe? Don't know. Don't care. I figure this has got to be better than where those other women were taken. They give me a little food and water, and I spend the day sleeping. No one has touched me."

Her eyes ran over Camila, taking in her expensive dress and shoes. "How'd you end up here? You don't seem like the type of woman they'd normally target."

"Horrible luck," Camila muttered. "And lots of enemies, apparently."

"I'll say. You'll probably be the next to go. They can make a pretty penny off someone like you." Her eyes ran over Camila again. "Unless they're holding you for ransom? Some rich boyfriend or husband to come rescue you?"

Camila's stomach tightened. "My father," she murmured.

The woman chuffed out a laugh. "Wonderful. A daddy's girl. You'll probably be out of here in no time then. Unless they can make more selling you to the highest bidder."

Camila pressed her lips together. The women who were sold as sex slaves were usually never seen again. But being held for ransom didn't mean she'd fare well either. Did they take her for money? Or to lure out her father?

He could pay a ransom, and it'd still be possible they'd never let her go.

Not when she was the bait that all those men would love to claim.

Her lower lip trembled, and she bit down into her flesh, refusing to give in to her despair. Refusing to give the men who'd taken her any of her tears. What had she just told Rosa the other day? She could take care of herself.

Inexplicably, her mind flashed back to Colton. His warm brown eyes, muscled hands, and commanding presence had soothed her in a way she didn't think was possible. Not when she'd never needed a man in her life before. Someone like him would always make sure she was safe and secure. A man like that would tear down walls and fight wars to get her back.

But right now?

She had no one on her side.

She wasn't his.

Her father would come—maybe. He'd send some of his men at least. But would that be more about saving face or rescuing her? And if he did show up or send a team in after her, would her captors really let her go?

"How long have I been here?" she asked the woman.

"Probably fifteen hours or so. They brought you here yesterday afternoon—the guy carrying you in wanted to rip your dress off you right here in front of everyone. The others wouldn't let him."

Camila shuddered.

"I guess you're too valuable for that. They haven't touched me yet either—can't pretend to know why. I don't know how many women are being held here. Most don't seem to stay very long. And the men running it like to sample the merchandise, if you know what I mean."

Camila muttered a curse as a woman a few feet away started sobbing. "I shouldn't be here!" she wailed. "I need to go home!"

"Shh, sweetheart," the woman clad in jeans said. "Don't let them hear you."

"What's your name?" Camila asked.

"Mariana. You?"

"Camila."

"Don't expect to get out of here," Mariana said. "One way or another—they own you now. It's easier to accept that."

"I'll never accept that," Camila said, disgusted.

Mariana shrugged. "Maybe you're lucky. You're rich. But the rest of us? We don't have a chance."

Chapter 8

Colton sank down into a seat on the C-17 cargo plane, dropping his duffle bag beside him. In his combat boots and fatigues, fueled by caffeine and power bars, he felt ready to take on the whole damn world. To track down the infamous drug lord *and* find the kingpin's daughter.

Wherever the hell they'd taken her.

Virginia Beach and Little Creek were far in the distance, thousands of feet down below them. The plane banked slightly to the right, the roar of the engines loud enough to briefly distract him from the thoughts running through his head.

Hunter grabbed the seat across from him, his anchor and snake tattoos peeking out beneath his white tee shirt as he moved. He tossed his camo shirt onto the empty seat in front of him, stretching out his legs.

"One nonstop flight to Bogota, coming up."

Colton smirked. "Not exactly a vacation."

"Ain't that the truth. Did you read that background briefing from the CO? About why cocaine production is up? The Colombian government reduced eradiation of the crop fields to have less fighting with the cartels. Less fighting but more drugs. That shit is fucked up."

Colton raised his eyebrows. "Guess it backfired. They're still fighting—just against each other instead of against the government."

"Hell, maybe that's what they wanted. Doesn't exactly bode well for the U.S. with the insane amounts of cocaine being smuggled in."

"Even if we nab Rodriguez, what the hell good does it do? Some other guy will just take over and run the operation."

"It sounds like they're hoping for answers. Bring him in, bring them all down."

"Yeah. Not sure that's exactly how it'll play out. And that sure as shit doesn't help all the innocent women they've taken."

"You're fucked," Hunter said, shooting Colton a knowing look.

"That's helpful," Colton muttered, grabbing his noise-cancelling headphones from his gear. Maybe Hunter would take the hint. He wasn't exactly in the mood to listen to the rest of the team banter. Between rushing to base for their early briefing, heading back home to grab his gear, and hauling ass back to deploy?

He'd barely had time to think, let alone consider all the repercussions of what was happening.

To be so damn close to Camila and unable to help her?

Not tasked to find her?

That shit was eating him alive.

The noise of the plane was a good distraction, but if it meant he'd have to listen to his teammates, he was more than willing to pull on his headphones, close his eyes, and deal with his innermost thoughts.

"We'll find her," Hunter assured him.

Colton stuffed his headphones back into his bag. "Don't see how," he said. "Those women that are kidnapped are shipped off all over the damn world. There's no telling where Camila is—she could be on the other side of the planet by now. All those surveillance devices I planted on her things in Miami don't help a damn now that she's missing. They left everything of hers behind in the café."

Hunter scrubbed a hand over his jaw. "Hell. You think they'd send off Miguel Rodriguez's only daughter? Sell her to the highest bidder?"

"How the hell should I know?" Colton asked.

"They've got plenty of women for that sort of seedy thing. An entire drug running operation built around it. This was an inside job, and they have him at their fucking mercy. Even a cold-hearted bastard like Miguel isn't about to let his daughter disappear into some sex-trafficking ring. And he sure as shit won't let her kidnappers hold her forever. Hell, even if he couldn't care less about her, it's about saving face. Keeping his image."

"Say he does go after her. What then? Our op is tracking down Miguel—taking him out if necessary. We find him and we're done."

"He's out there looking for his daughter. We'll kill two birds with one stone."

Colton muttered a curse. "And what about all the other women there? You think we can just grab

Camila if we find her and stroll on out? Leave them in harm's way?"

Ryker moved down the aisle of the cargo plane, his large frame sinking down into a seat by Colton and Hunter. "You know where I stand on this," he said in a low voice, leaning forward with determination written across his face as he eyed them. "You know where the entire team stands—we're not leaving innocent women in the hands of those assholes. If we find them, they're coming with us."

"Shit," Hunter muttered. "Not sure how we're supposed to move out a ton of women. Our team's rolling in on two Humvees. Not that I'd leave them there either."

"Who else is down there?" Colton asked.

"The hell if I know. DEA agents were tracking him for months. Following the drug money. Gathering intel on his inner circle. It sounded like there are just a few agents left down there now though. As for grabbing him? We're it. He's been spotted out in the open, so the Pentagon gave the go ahead."

"That's why we're moving in. We know. It still doesn't help me a damn bit in finding Camila."

"I know how you feel," Hunter said. "They took Emma, remember? I brought her home with me, and they fucking grabbed her."

Colton frowned. Hunter had met the British archeologist during a brief trip to London earlier in the year. He and Mason had happened to be in the right place at the right time when she'd bumped into him in a pub. When she'd eventually returned to the U.S. with Hunter and terrorists had still tracked her down, Hunter had been the one to rescue her.

It didn't make his own situation any damn easier though.

Hell. He barely even knew Camila, but the thought of her in harm's way, being held against her will, had him seeing red.

"Shit," he muttered.

Hunter raised his eyebrows.

"I only spent one night with her, and I can't get her out of my head. The thought that she could've been hurt, or raped, or worse—it just fucking kills me."

Ryker smirked. "You, my friend, are totally fucked. She must have been some woman to have you wrapped around her finger like this. You're as bad as Hunter now."

Hunter briefly chuckled before grabbing his gear beside his seat. "You think I'm going to complain about having Emma in my bed every night? Not a fucking chance. I'm going over the maps again. We'll probably have new intel by the time we land, but I want to be intimately familiar with the terrain we'll be dealing with. Hell. Once we grab Miguel, maybe he'll have some leads on where they took his daughter."

"Do we still think he's somewhere in the city?"

"Affirmative. But as for how long that'll last? Not a damn clue. Not if he's out searching for his daughter. And if it's true that they're trying to run him out of town, he could be damn well anywhere."

"Wonderful," Colton murmured, grabbing his headphones from his bag again.

"I gotta rest up, too," Ryker said. "I wasn't expecting an extra early wake-up call."

Hunter eyed him in amusement. "Did you even get the name of the woman you left in bed this morning?"

"Nope," he said with a chuckle.

Colton shook his head in disbelief, putting on his headphones. He leaned back against the uncomfortable seat, shutting his eyes. Letting the darkness take over.

Thoughts whirled through his mind, and he clenched his fists.

There was nothing like being so powerful, part of goddamn Navy SEAL team with weapons and equipment and whatever they needed at their disposal, yet feeling so helpless at the same time.

Chapter 9

The plane descended into a remote area outside of Bogota, coming to a stop at the end of a bumpy dirt runway. DEA had left some equipment around for their flights in and out, and members of the Colombian military had been guarding the site now that the Delta team was arriving.

Colton strode down the metal ramp of the C-17 cargo plane, gear on his back, assault rifle in hand, and into the cool South American air. Although it was the start of spring in the southern hemisphere, the elevation of the city made it cooler than other parts of Colombia. Not to mention a nice damn change from the 100-degree desert heat. They'd been wheels-up to the Middle East more times in recent years than he could count.

Stunning expanses of dark mountains and blue sky filled the horizon, and he stopped, scanning his surroundings. Taking a breath of the cool, refreshing air. At the moment, Colombia looked nothing but peaceful and serene.

Save for the rival drug cartels battling one another, the kidnapping ring run by Camila's father, and the other hidden dangers waiting for them.

The presence of the military surrounding the remote airstrip proved it was anything but calm and quiet.

"Hell of a change from the desert air," Noah said as he came up beside him, sliding on his aviators.

Colton glanced off in the distance, to the members of the Colombian military at the other end of the runway. "Yeah. I hate to say it, but I like the break from all that damn heat. Doesn't mean I like the reason we were sent down here though."

His eyes narrowed as he looked around. Imprints from combat boots were left in the dusty ground, and their plane had left tire tracks where it had come to a stop at the end of the runway. Other vehicles' tire tracks circled the area, no doubt from the DEA agents and Colombian military.

Uncle Sam had the DEA coming and going for months in an attempt to track down the notorious drug lord. Amazing that in a way, the kidnapping of his daughter had helped to flush him out. Storming his compound could've been an option requiring a hell of a lot more firepower. Grabbing him when he was with a small group of his own men would make it practically too damn easy.

And now that he was out in the open?

Their perfect chance had come at the cost of Camila's kidnapping.

The sound of boots on metal from another SEAL team member walking down the C-17 ramp had Colton glancing back behind him. Hunter dropped his gear on the ground, holding only his weapon, and scanned the distance. "There's a hell of a lot of places to hide in the mountains. The latest word was that Miguel was still in the city though. We'll set up base here with extra supplies. Go over the specs again. We roll into the city at nightfall unless we receive new information. Grab him from the location he was last spotted at and bring him back to the States."

"Understood," Colton said, clenching his jaw. His hand fisted at his side, and he gripped his assault rifle more tightly.

Situations were always rapidly changing. New developments unfolding. They could easily hunt down Miguel and leave without ever spotting one of the missing women.

Without Camila.

Ryker spat on the ground as he strode over, coming to a stop beside them. His dark hair gleamed in the sunlight, and he adjusted his headset and nodded toward some recently disturbed earth less than fifty yards from them.

"What the hell is that?" Colton asked, his eyes narrowing.

"Hidden drugs? Money? A recently-dug grave? Don't know. It could be anything."

Colton's blood ran cold. He took a step toward it, his gaze instinctively sweeping the area. "It doesn't look like explosives. It would be hard to sneak in and plant them anyway with so many eyes in the area."

"Well something sure as shit has been there," Ryker comment dryly.

Hunter moved up beside Colton, taking command. "Colton and I will check out the disturbance," he said into his headset. "Ryker and Noah, wait here until the other members of team disembark the plane. The Colombians will be rolling up in a few minutes."

Ryker's gaze slid to the waiting plane. "Roger that," he said, casually looking around.

A military vehicle starting driving toward them from the other end of the airstrip.

"We're gathering up some additional gear," Jacob said over the comm channel. "About to unload the Humvees from the plane. You guys see something out there?"

"It looks like something's buried in the ground nearby," Hunter said. "Someone. Hell, it could be nothing. We'll find out in fifty yards."

"Roger that," Jacob said coolly. Metal clanked in the background, and Colton heard an engine start.

He looked into the distance, knowing the rest of their men had him covered from behind. That the military at the far end of the runway would most likely ward off potential attacks. There was nothing else around but an open field of dirt in the area between the city and mountains. There weren't many places for someone to hide. That didn't mean someone couldn't launch an RPG their way though. Or plant an IED in the ground.

The cartels weren't likely to bring the war to them, not on an airstrip guarded by the Colombian military. They had their own turf wars against each other— their own caco fields to guard. Their own cocaine shipments to protect.

Colton's eyes trailed over the brown dirt. Aside from tire tracks and boot imprints, both lessening the further away they walked, nothing around here appeared to be recently disturbed.

"See anything suspicious?" Hunter asked, his eyes

sweeping the area.

"Negative. Let's keep alert as we move forward. The cartels are known to have IEDs. Seems unlikely they'd come here though."

"Affirmative. The cartels won't come out here looking for a fight. Doesn't mean some lone wolf won't see us and decide to shoot."

"Game on," Colton muttered.

Static crackled over his headset, and their CO's voice from Little Creek filled his ear. "Delta team— we've received new intelligence while you were midflight. Miguel Rodriguez was spotted in a convoy of vehicles heading west of the city at 1700 local time. Coordinates are on the way."

"Roger that," Hunter said quietly into his headset. "We're investigating what looks to be a buried body at the edge of the airfield, and then we'll be on the move. The Colombians can investigate further and deal with it. We're just making sure someone wasn't buried alive out here."

"Roger. Over and out," their CO said.

Colton and Hunter approached the mound of dirt slowly, cautiously edging closer. Colton paused, looking at the ground. Dirt covered his combat boots. All the tire tracks left on the ground meant that it hadn't rained recently. Which meant it would've been harder to dig a grave.

Someone could've dumped a body and then just piled dirt atop it, not even bothering to make sure they were six feet underground.

"It hasn't rained recently," Colton said. "Maybe that's why whatever they buried isn't very deep? A freshly-dug mound of dirt sure as hell doesn't conceal the location at all though."

"You think there are explosives buried around here?" Hunter asked.

Colton paused, glancing around. There were no tell-tale signs of a tripwire, but IEDs were generally well hidden because they were so small. "I doubt anyone would bury a large explosive device way out here," he said, nodding in the direction of the mound. "If they wanted to target a plane, it would need to be on the runway. And with the military standing guard, it'd be difficult to get close enough for that."

"Agreed. Maybe they dumped a body. It's not exactly a great location to hide cash or drugs."

The walked closer to the pile of fresh dirt, and Colton's heart dropped as he saw a woman's shoe abandoned on the ground. A sprinkling of dirt covered the pink sandal, and the delicate strap was broken.

"Shit," Hunter muttered beside him. "Definite corpse. Looks like it was recently buried."

Unable to stop himself, Colton stepped closer. He ground his jaw as he saw strands of blonde hair and realized that his heart had been thumping wildly. That he'd inadvertently been holding his breath.

It wasn't Camila.

But another young woman had lost her life. Probably kidnapped by the cartels and then tossed aside. Accidentally killed, perhaps. Maybe left to send a message.

And now she was abandoned in the dirt.

"Strange to leave a body way out here," Hunter mused, glancing around. "If they wanted the military to find it, past the end of the runway doesn't seem like a great choice."

"DEA has been flying planes in and out of this

area for months," Colton said. "It does seem risky to come all the way out here just to dump a body. Not when the U.S. has boots on the ground. Maybe this was as close as they could get and hope that the U.S. or Colombian military would find it."

"All right boys, enough talk about the damn body," Ryker said over the headsets. "The sat imagery we just received shows exactly where Miguel's convoy stopped. No telling how long it'll be before they move out again. I'm pulling up the specs, and we can be on our merry way."

"Hell." Hunter glanced again at the pile of dirt covering the woman before looking back toward their C-17 and teammates. The rest of the team was gathered around the Humvees, packing up the rest of the gear. Nothing like landing with their own vehicles ready to roll.

"She'll still be here when we get back," Colton said.

Hunter nodded, turning and walking toward the rest of the team.

"What'd you find?" their CO asked over the headsets. "Anything to be concerned about?"

"A woman's body. Tell the Colombians to investigate further after we move out. Colton and I are headed back to Delta."

Colton followed behind, uneasiness settling over him. Something didn't sit right about a body being dumped here, in an area the U.S. Government was known to frequent.

Someone was sending them a message.

But what?

Chapter 10

Camila gasped as rough hands lifted her up, rousing her from a groggy sleep. She stumbled as a man pushed her forward, bodily dragging her from the room. Her weakened state was no match for his bulk and muscle, and she could do little but let him take her.

Thick fingers gripped her biceps as he moved her toward the door, sending pain shooting down her arms. The woman who'd been wailing on her own mat earlier whimpered, but no one said a word. She frantically scanned the room, as if the small cell of women could somehow save her from her captor.

She briefly met the frightened eyes of Mariana but knew there was nothing the woman could do to help her either. If anything, it was better they were taking Camila. At least she had a chance of eventually escaping—of being rescued. Presumably, they'd contact her father for money. And if they did intend to sell her into the sex trade like those other women, word would spread quickly that the daughter of Miguel Rodriguez was up for sale.

She shuddered, looking ahead.

Pretending she wasn't leaving the other women in the room behind for a miserable life as the property of a man willing to pay.

Camila blinked as she nearly fell into the narrow hallway, dimly lit by a few lights. It was made of the same concrete cinderblocks as the cell she'd been hidden in. Dark. Narrow. Unwelcoming.

And perfect for hiding whatever goods they were trafficking.

Whatever they'd drugged her with had mostly worn off, but she was weak from no food or water, and she swayed on her feet. She shivered in her dress and sandals, uneasiness washing over her.

How many more hours had passed since she'd been taken?

Were they dragging her off to rape or kill her?

Her stomach lurched, and she dry heaved, glancing down at the boots of the man holding her. He smelled of cigarettes and stale sweat, and he pulled her along, not caring if she was about to be sick.

"We have to move her," another man yelled impatiently. Camila glanced up to see the shadow of another man at the end of the hallway. "If he discovers she's being held here, he'll slit our throats."

"What? Where are we going?" she asked the man holding her, finally getting up the nerve to speak.

He grunted, shoving her forward, and she nearly fell to the ground. Rough hands yanked her back into a standing position, and then he was hurrying her along. Camila's eyes widened as she saw pounds and pounds of cocaine being stacked into piles as they passed an open storage room. There had to be millions and millions of dollars' worth of drugs in that one tiny little space.

The men working ignored her, too caught up in their assignment to care.

Or maybe they were just used to seeing women taken in and out of the cell where she'd been held.

Were they clearing out their stash of cocaine? Was this part of her father's operations? Or something run by another cartel?

She hadn't seen her own bodyguards since they'd been outside the café—right after they'd turned on her. Crazy how two men who'd protected her for years suddenly were willing to sell her out. Was this a building owned by her father? Or had they given her to a rival cartel?

A rickety door at the end of the hallway revealed a set of concrete stairs, and before she could ask any more questions or refuse to go up, the man holding her heaved her up over his shoulder.

She screamed as his arm snaked around her waist, holding her to him, and his other hand palmed her ass as he chuckled. He squeezed her buttocks lightly, and she screamed again, kicking her legs.

"Quiet!" the man holding her shouted. He smacked her ass once, shocking her, and she let out a sob as he began hissing at her to shut up.

"Want me to take care of her?" the man who'd been waiting at the end of the hallway asked. "Twenty minutes alone with me will shut her the fuck up. I'll stuff my cock so deep in her mouth, she'll be gagging too much to even think about screaming."

"We need her alive," the guy holding her snapped.

A dark chuckle had her cringing. "I was going fuck

her, not kill her."

"Later."

Her head bounced up and down against her captor's back as he carried her up the stairs, and she began to feel sickeningly dizzy. Soon she felt the cool night air kissing the backs of her legs. Chilling her exposed skin. As her eyes adjusted to the darkness, she realized that hours had passed since she'd first woken.

Was it really only one day ago that she'd been kidnapped from the café?

She'd been shopping and having coffee with her best friend—not a single care in the world. It was amazing how in such a short time her world had been turned upside down—both literally and figuratively.

The guy holding her over his shoulder unceremoniously lifted her off and dumped her onto the ground. She scurried back as the man who'd been hidden in shadows walked over to them. Tattoos covered both of his muscular arms, and he had several days growth of a dark beard. The outline of a packet of cigarettes showed in his shirt pocket, but in the cool night air, he didn't reek of the scent of stale smoke like the first man had.

Dark eyes flickered over her with interest, lingering on her breasts. Chilling her to the core. Her nipples pressed against the fabric of her thin dress, pebbling from the cold, and she could practically see his mouth watering.

"It's a damn shame I couldn't take you for a test ride," he said with a smirk, reaching out and lightly caressing one of her breasts as she pulled away. "Maybe they'll let me try you out later. After your buyer gets his fill of you."

She let out a choked cry and trembled as a dark van pulled up the driveway. Three men in dark clothes climbed out, storming over to her and the tattooed man. Each of them were carrying weapons, and one glanced back over his shoulder at the idling vehicle, a driver still waiting inside. "Miguel's on the move," one of them said. "Rumor has it he's on his way here."

Camila's ears perked up. Her father was coming to rescue her? She stood perfectly still, hoping they didn't realize she was listening to the conversation.

"How could he know where she is?" the tattooed man snapped. He reached into his pocket and pulled out a packet of cigarettes, lighting one. The soft glow of the embers lit up in the darkness, and she tried not to retch at the smell. At the nausea she was feeling after not eating for more than twenty-four hours. "He's got property all over Colombia. What the hell would let him know we've taken over this compound?"

"He killed one of her bodyguards. The fools came back demanding a bigger ransom for his daughter after they kidnapped her. The second one was willing to talk after the first lost his life."

"Fuck. Where is he now?"

"The bodyguard? Both are dead."

Camila took a step back, her eyes widening. The tattooed man reached out and yanked her back toward him, the ashes from his cigarette falling onto her bare skin. "I'll be coming for you later, beautiful." She winced as his fingers gripped her wrist tightly, binding her to him.

"Who are you?" she demanded.

She tried to wrench her wrist free from his grip,

and he chuckled. "Just an old rival of your father's. Remember that massive fire a year ago? Your father torched our caco crops—it cost me millions. But I'm about to get my revenge."

Camila stared up at him, a feeling of dread washing over her. Was he planning to kill her father? Her? Attempt to take over the entire cartel?

If her bodyguards had already been killed, how much chance did this man have? Her father already knew what was happening.

"And what do you need me for?" she asked, raising her chin defiantly.

He chuckled. "We're in the same business as your father—moving drugs and women. I'm having a special auction just for you though. Usually men don't care what whore they end up with when we sell them. A warm cunt is all they need," he sneered as she shivered.

"I've taken a woman or two myself over the years. Reaped the benefits of this business. But you?" he asked, slowly circling around her. Examining every inch of her in the darkness.

She shivered, despite her efforts to remain still. To not quake in front of the group of men before her. "The daughter of the infamous Miguel Rodriguez? Your father cost me millions, but I'm about to make it all back. There are lots of men willing to fuck the likes of you. They'll pay big money for the chance. Hell, maybe I'll sell you for a night at a time."

"No," she said, taking a step back. "I won't do it."

"You'll do whatever the fuck I tell you," he snarled. "Hell. I'll fuck you right here myself in front of all these other men—then let them each have a turn."

He nodded at the men from the van, and two of them began walking toward her.

"No!" she shouted, turning to run. Stumbling in the dark as she blindly took off. After only a few steps they were grabbing her by the arms. Lifting her into the air. She screamed again, twisting and writhing as she tried to break free.

"Knock her out," a dark voice commanded.

She cried out again as something hard hit the top of her head, and then she succumbed to the darkness.

Chapter 11

The city grew larger as they sped toward it, the Humvee bouncing along the dirt road. Colton rode shotgun as Jacob drove, Ryker in the seat behind them. Colton clenched his jaw, glancing back at the outline of the mountains in the distance. A sliver of moon shone in the sky above them. He adjusted his night-vision goggles.

Hell.

Camila was still out there somewhere. Kidnapped. Alone.

Given the reports that her father was in a convoy leaving the city, it was pretty damn likely she wasn't with him. His SEAL team would grab the package and be on their merry-fucking-way, one nonstop flight back to Little Creek.

And if Camila was left behind, frightened and at the mercy of her captors?

Not their damn problem, according to the Pentagon.

Jacob glanced over at Colton from his spot behind the steering wheel. "This op reminds me of when we rushed the terrorist camp in Afghanistan—nightfall, a missing woman. A group of assholes thinking they rule the world with no fucking idea that we're coming."

"Except Camila's not with her father. We're just grabbing the Rodriguez cartel's kingpin and getting the hell out of Dodge. Last time we knew the exact location of the missing woman. Hell—last time our op *was* the missing woman."

"Yeah, well, a senator's daughter is a little different than the daughter of a drug lord. Especially in the eyes of the U.S. government."

Ryker leaned forward from his spot in the back of the Humvee. "What'd Hunter say? You know he wouldn't want to leave her behind."

"Hell. What can he do?" Colton asked. "We have orders from the CO straight from the Pentagon. It's not like we can drive all over Bogota looking for the woman I had a one-night-stand with. We don't even have a damn fucking clue where she is."

Jacob grunted in affirmation. "There's a vehicle coming our way," he said into the mouthpiece of his headset.

Hunter's voice came through their earpieces from the other Humvee. "Roger that. Looks to be like a civilian vehicle. Don't slow down. The highway is coming up in one hundred yards. We'll loop around the outskirts of the city and intercept the convoy. Last known location was five miles outside of Bogota."

Colton's gaze swept the area, his assault rifle clenched in his hands. The car approaching them on the other side of the dirt road drove right by them without incident. He glanced back over his shoulder, watching it continue down the road and eventually go out of sight.

"Do we have an update on which vehicle Miguel's believed to be in?" Jacob asked into his mouthpiece.

"Negative," Hunter responded. "The CO is getting additional sat imagery as we speak. Appears to be four vehicles, possibly a fifth trailing in the distance."

"We're approximately ten minutes out from their location," Jacob said.

"Roger that," Hunter said in a cool voice. "We'll head off the front vehicle of the convoy if we don't have confirmation on which one the target is. Noah and Jacob, remain in the Humvees unless it all goes to hell. This is just a snatch and grab. As soon as we have hands on Miguel, we're out."

"I wonder what the supposed additional vehicle is?" Jacob asked the others in his Humvee.

"Another cartel tailing them?" Ryker asked.

"Possibly," Colton agreed. "It could be them; it could be nothing. There's lots of traffic on the main highway."

Their CO's voice suddenly came over their headsets. "The new images were just sent to you. It looks like the target is riding in the fourth vehicle."

"We'll ambush them from the sides," Hunter said. "Don't worry about the first three vehicles. We go in, grab the package, and get out."

"Roger that," the other men said.

There was a bump as the Humvee left the dirt road and pulled onto the highway. Jacob accelerated, speeding toward the convoy. "ETA is one minute," he said in a low voice. "Let's do this."

"We'll cover the left side, you take the right,"

Hunter commanded. "Let's cut him off and take him in."

They sped along the side of the highway, racing ahead of the other traffic, until Colton could see four vehicles traveling together up ahead.

"Target in in sight," Jacob said, his hands gripping the steering wheel. "Fourth vehicle is a dark SUV. Looks like tinted windows. No telling which seat Miguel's in."

"Roger that," Noah said over the headsets. "I'll meet you up there."

"Who's that coming up behind us?" Ryker asked, twisting to look behind them.

A car speeding out of nowhere suddenly weaved back and forth between the other traffic and accelerated ahead of them. "He's got someone hanging outside of the window," Colton said. "Make that something. Looks like a rocket launcher."

"A fucking rocket launcher?" Hunter asked in disbelief. "Since when did the cartels start using those?"

"Since now," Colton said, his voice grim.

The whiz of an RPG suddenly raced through the night sky, exploding into the fourth car in the convoy. The SUV burst into a ball of fire as it flew through the air, the other cars in the convoy speeding up to escape the explosion.

"Fuck!" Jacob shouted, swerving to avoid the fiery blast.

Debris filled the air around them, thumping against the side of the Humvee. Colton crouched in his seat, muttering a curse. Noah swerved the other Humvee in a different direction, until both vehicles screeched to a stop at the side of the highway, a safe distance ahead of the massive fire.

"Damn it!" their CO shouted over the headsets. "Someone else was trying to take him out. Is anyone getting out of the target's vehicle? Are there any survivors? Move in!"

Colton and Ryker jumped out of their Humvee, with Hunter and Mason climbing out of the second. "Move forward!" Hunter commanded, and the men began running toward the wreckage. "Keep eyes on the other vehicles as well!"

Colton scanned back and forth, the scene before him clear through his night-vision goggles. Other traffic had stopped, and people were climbing out of their own vehicles, cell phones in hands. Some shouted in disbelief while others held their hands up to their faces in horror. Sirens sounded in the distance, and smoke filled the air.

The wreckage of the SUV blazed against the night sky, the smell of explosives and burning metal permeating the cool air.

"That was a hell of a lot of firepower to take out a damn SUV!" Hunter shouted over the roar of the flames.

The charred black vehicle could be seen through the inferno, and Colton muttered a curse. "There's no way there are any survivors!" he yelled.

The sound of helicopters filled the air, and Colton glanced skyward to see the Colombian military in the distance.

"So much for taking that mother fucker back with us," Hunter said. "Let's move out!"

The men jogged back to the idling Humvees, climbing inside the vehicles. "We're heading back to the airstrip," Hunter said over the headsets.

"Affirmative," their CO said. "I'll have additional instructions once you arrive back there."

"Damn it!" Colton said, pounding his fist against the dashboard. "God damn it!"

Jacob maneuvered the Humvee around the wreckage as fire trucks approached, driving right over the grassy highway median to head back on the opposite side of the highway to the air field. Noah followed behind in the second Humvee, and some of the cars now stuck in the traffic jam on the highway started trying to follow them across the median as well.

"Wait!" Ryker yelled from the back of the vehicle. "What's that lying in the grass?"

Colton's gaze swept the area outside the window through his night-vision goggles, finally noticing what looked to be a messenger bag, its contents scattered around. His eyes narrowed as he noticed a laptop lying amidst the debris.

"That can't be from the SUV that exploded," Ryker said in disbelief, his voice low. "There's no fucking way."

"What do you see?" Hunter asked over the headsets.

"A messenger bag. Laptop. Other personal belongings." Colton's voice was clipped.

"It must be from one of the other vehicles that sped away when Miguel's SUV was hit," Hunter said, the Humvee he was riding in pulling up beside them. "Maybe even that damn car with the rocket launcher. That asshole was hanging out the car window. When they swerved and sped away, it could've flown out."

"I'll grab it," Colton said, his hand already on the door. He clutched his assault rifle in one hand and climbed out of the Humvee. He strode over to the contents scattered on the ground, nudging the edge of the messenger bag with his combat boot. "Probably a mistake that it got left behind," he said in a low voice over his headset. "I can't imagine they'd leave this type of thing on purpose. I don't see any wires or explosives."

"Let's bring it in," Hunter said.

Colton stuffed the materials into the torn messenger bag, his gloved hand lightly running over the laptop. If whoever had left this behind was indeed who'd taken out Miguel Rodriguez, they might also be the one who'd taken Miguel's daughter. Which meant information critical to finding her could be right at his fingertips.

His heartbeat accelerated as adrenaline pumped through his veins. The *thump, thump, thump* of helicopters filled the air as the Colombian military got closer to the scene of the explosion. So much for keeping quiet on their operation to grab Miguel. The whole damn world would know about it soon.

CNN and the other news networks would be running it as breaking news.

They needed to get the hell out before their faces were splashed across the nighttime news.

"Shit," he muttered to himself, stuffing the laptop into the bag. He hurried back to the Humvee, slamming the door behind him. The headlights cut through the darkness as they pulled forward, rolling onto the highway back to the airstrip.

Police had stopped traffic coming from the opposite direction to grant access to all the emergency vehicles converging on the scene, and they had the highway to themselves.

"Are you thinking what I'm thinking?" Jacob asked, glancing over at Colton in the passenger seat of the Humvee.

"Hell yeah. The answers we need to find Camila might have fallen right into our hands."

"Let's get back to base and fire that thing up," Ryker said. "We've got more work to do."

Chapter 12

Camila fell to the side of the van she was riding in as it lurched to the left, banging her head against the wall. Pain smarted through her temple, wrapping around her entire head, and she was certain a bruise would be forming soon. She struggled against the ropes binding her wrists and ankles, trying to sit back up. Desperate to see what was happening around her despite the darkness.

The man left to guard her in the back of the van had been leering at her for the entire ride, his face lit only by the glow of his cell phone and cigarette. Suddenly he was moving toward her. Over her.

She screamed as he grabbed her arms, but he roughly pulled her back into a sitting position, shoving her against the wall, and then crouched down back where he'd been.

He glanced down at his cell phone as it began to vibrate, then frowned as he saw the message on the screen. Screaming in Spanish, he slammed it down, seeming unconcerned if he smashed it altogether. The van skidded to an abrupt stop, tires screeching, and then the back doors were suddenly pulled open.

She cringed against the bright lights of the flashlights aimed at her, for a brief moment hoping she'd been rescued. Two of the men dressed in black climbed in and grabbed her, hauling her outside of the van to the side of the highway.

She swayed between them, her bound legs leaving her unable to do much of anything.

"Let's leave her here," one of the men snapped. "We can come back later if need be. This is getting out of hand. The entire scenario revolved around him coming!"

"Damn it all to hell," a second man said, kicking the ground. He threw his cigarette down, smashing it beneath his foot. In an instant he was coming toward Camila. He pulled a large knife from a pocket of his pants, tossing the sheath onto the ground. She screamed as he moved toward her, but he suddenly ducked down, gripping one of her calves as he cut the rope binding her ankles. He stood back up, towering above her. Before she could ask any questions, his fingers wrapped around her bicep, and he began painfully dragging her through a field.

She stumbled in the darkness, her ankles raw and sore from where the rope had bound her. It still cut into her wrists, but she didn't dare ask for him to free her arms, too.

Rows and rows of caco grew all around them, and she looked around in confusion as they trampled through the plants. He moved in a strange zig-zag pattern, and she went with him, bewildered.

They were dumping her in a field? What happened

to the auction? Was he taking her out here alone to rape or kill her?

The plants brushed and scratched against her bare legs, and she stumbled over a pile of dirt, still wearing her heeled sandals. If she ever escaped from any of this, she was burning her entire outfit—both her dress and shoes. She didn't want any reminder of what she'd been through.

To her astonishment, the sound of helicopters filled the air in the distance, and she could see an eerie orange glow in the night sky.

"What's going on? Is something on fire over there?"

"It seems that another cartel took out your father tonight. The SUV he was riding in exploded on impact."

"What?" she gasped. "You're lying."

"Not lying. It's a pity, really, since we were planning to collect millions from him. Now that he's gone, we have to reschedule your auction. And I can't risk us being stopped and having you taken from us for free. I'm leaving you out here until things settle down."

"In the middle of a field?" she asked, suddenly feeling exhausted. The brief rush of adrenaline when she'd been pulled from the van was fading, any hopes of a rescue disappearing.

"I promised my men that Miguel would pay up. Come and give us a hefty ransom for his only daughter. The allure of you would have men bidding higher at the auction than we ever imagined. Of course, I was anticipating your father being forced to bid for your freedom as well," he said with a dark chuckle. "I'll be back to gather you shortly."

He turned and began to walk away, leaving her standing there alone in the darkness. Was this some kind of sick joke? Was he going to come back a few minutes later and kill her? As soon as he was out of sight she was going to run. To never look back.

He stopped when he'd gotten only a few feet away. She could see his silhouette in the darkness but sensed he was looking back at her. "This entire field is rigged with IEDS—improvised explosive devices. It's to keep the government from ruining our fields. And to keep men like your father from burning them to the ground. One wrong step, and you'll blow your leg right off. It'll be harder to run when you're injured. Don't move until I come back for you."

Camila shivered as he walked away, her stomach dropping. This had to be some sort of nightmare. He kidnapped her just to leave her in a damn field that he claimed was rigged with explosives?

The door to the van slammed shut, startling her, and then with a roar of the engine it was speeding off into the darkness.

Smoke billowed in the sky in the distance, cast in that sickly orange glow from the flames. Was it really her father who'd been killed? Or were they just saying that to frighten her?

The cool night air nipped at her bare flesh, and suddenly the gravity of the past few days washed over her. She was exhausted. Hungry. Thirsty. Freezing.

Should she run away?

Try to get help?

There was no telling if what her captor had said was in fact true or if he was simply trying to frighten her by claiming the entire field was rigged with explosives. He'd somehow moved through it, although in that odd zig-zag pattern.

She sank to the ground, yawning despite herself. She needed to run. Hide. Take whatever chances with his claims about the IEDs. Nothing would be worse than being auctioned off to a group of men. Than being sold and treated as some man's property for the rest of her life.

Her legs felt weak as she tried to stand, her bound arms doing little to help her, and then she fell back to the hard ground and surrendered to the darkness.

Chapter 13

Colton drummed his fingers on the makeshift table, his gaze scanning over the emails on the laptop. Uneasiness filled his chest, and his eyes ran over the subject lines, hoping they could find something, anything, that would lead them to Camila.

Searching the whole damn city of Bogota wasn't exactly an option—not when there was no telling when or if they'd ever find her.

Hunter hunched over the laptop screen, the rest of the team crowded around behind him. "Fuck, these guys are idiots. They didn't even try to encrypt anything," Hunter said, scrolling through more of the messages.

Ryker smirked. "That's what makes them idiots? How about losing their damn laptop in the middle of a highway? Half of Bogota probably drives right by there. They take out the head of the Rodriguez cartel and then leave behind a laptop outlining their entire operation? Fucking amateurs."

Mason chuckled. "Amateurs bringing in millions. Hell. Probably half of the drugs flowing into the U.S. are grown right here."

Hunter clicked on another message, and images of multiple maps of the Colombian caco fields filled the screen. "Shit. That's heavy duty stuff," Noah murmured. "Do you see how much they're growing? That's a hell of a lot of product to turn."

"And we don't even know how much Rodriguez controlled. This is the rival cartel's fields."

"Is the Colombian military going to want us to turn the laptop over to them?" Colton asked.

"Possibly. Probably. Our op was focused on Rodriguez," Hunter said. "Let's see if there's anything useful here before we hand it over. We can copy the files and go over the data with a fine-tooth comb later. Send it back to the States for the analysts to review."

"There," Colton suddenly said, pointing a finger at the screen. "There's an email about a special auction with today's date. Open that one."

"Shit," Ryker said, his eyes widening as Hunter clicked on the message. "They're auctioning off women?"

"That's why so many women in Colombia have gone missing," Hunter confirmed. "They sell them off to whoever can pay the price. It looks like this was a special event though."

"Fucking hell," Colton spat out. "A special event to auction off a person?"

"Easy," Hunter said. "I just mean it's not their usual method of delivery. They can traffic more women by just selling them off to the first buyer available. The auction was for Camila."

"Method of delivery," Colton muttered. "We're talking about people. A woman!"

"It was supposed to be tonight," Hunter said, scrolling to the bottom. "Whatever this is, we've got an entire list of contacts that the email was sent to. Let's upload the info and send it back to Little Creek. We'll turn over the laptop to the Colombian military, but we'll have a copy of all of the data on it. Names, emails, records—everything."

"Roger that," Noah said, plugging an external hard drive into the laptop. "I can copy everything in minutes. I'll upload the files and keep the backup myself."

Hunter met Colton's gaze. "This was supposed to go down tonight. That may have been shot to hell by them taking out Miguel, but there's a chance we can find your woman."

Colton nodded, his mouth pressed together in a thin line. Adrenaline raced through him, and he had the urge to beat the hell out of the first cartel member he spotted. To pound to a pulp any man who had done Camila harm.

And as to what, if anything, had happened while she'd been taken?

They'd deal with that when the time came.

"Let's do it," he said. "We'll show up to the site of the auction and see if anyone else does. Not everyone will know that Miguel was killed tonight. If this goes like we want it to, they'll bring Camila right to us."

"Hell," Noah said, eyeing him with interest. "What's she going to think when you come in guns blazing? Did you tell her what you do?"

"Negative," Colton said. "I'll worry about that once we have her. Until then? Rescuing her is my only concern."

Hunter spoke into his mouthpiece, connecting with their CO back in Little Creek. "We've looked over the data we found on the laptop and are copying the files. There's a chance we can rescue Camila Rodriguez. We're going after her," Hunter said.

"Negative. Stand down," their CO commanded.

"She might have information on her father," Hunter said, eyeing Colton. "On the entire operation. If another cartel took her, she's seen some of their operations from the inside, too. Since grabbing Miguel is out of the question now that he's been killed, and we don't have names yet for the rest of his inner circle, this is our shot. Grabbing her is just the tip of the iceberg."

"Damn it," their CO muttered. "This wasn't part of the assignment."

"Gathering intel on the Rodriguez cartel was though. Now that he's gone, she might be able to give us names of who else to look at. Not only can she potentially tell us about her father's cartel, but she'll hopefully also have descriptions of the other cartel's members. Whoever grabbed her was in competition with her father."

Their CO cursed through the headsets. "Fine. Move forward. Bring her in and get the hell out. I'll attempt to smooth things over with the Colombians. We can't just go around taking civilians without going through the proper diplomatic channels."

"Taking her?" Hunter chuckled. "We're rescuing her."

"Affirmative," their CO growled. "Move in."

"Yes, sir," Hunter said. "We'll be moving out immediately. Over and out."

Colton let out a breath he didn't realize he'd been holding. He paced the room, his mind spinning with scenarios of how this could play out. Grab her before she was brought in to the auction? Bust in and take down everyone there?

Show up and find the entire plan was for naught?

"You got the specs?" Jacob asked, crossing his arms as he looked over to where Hunter and Noah were still working at the laptop.

"Yep. The address was in the email," Hunter confirmed. "They might as well have sent us an engraved invitation."

Jacob grinned. "Let's go pay them a visit then, and get Colton back his girl."

Hunter closed the laptop, carrying it in one large hand to the Colombian military members hovering by the front door. "We're headed back out," he said, handing over the laptop. "We've got one more stop to make before we go wheels-up."

The men nodded as Hunter and his team cleared the room. Colton clenched his assault rifle, moving back into the darkness and hopping into the Humvee.

He had a woman to rescue.

***

Ryker pulled up the specs on the handheld GPS device, navigating from the back of the Humvee. "ETA is fifteen minutes from now. No telling if the auction is still on for later though. We might arrive and find nothing."

"Let's hope you're wrong," Colton murmured from the front.

"Yep. I hope to hell that I am," Ryker said. "If we

don't grab her tonight she might be gone. Permanently."

"What the hell is that?" Colton asked, watching as a van swerved down the highway in front of them.

"A couple of drunks?" Jacob guessed, easing up on the gas.

"Hell. We don't have time for this shit," Colton muttered. "Pull to the right so they can get by."

The van straightened out and sped past them, and Colton scanned the road around them with his night-vision goggles. Some of the fields to the right side of the road looked like they'd been recently trampled on. "Slow down," he said, glancing out the window. "It looks like they may have been over there." He pointed as Jacob pulled to a stop on the side of the highway.

All three of them exited the Humvee, notifying Hunter over their headsets.

"Roger that," Hunter said. "We'll continue to the original rendezvous point. Investigate whatever you spotted and meet us there ASAP."

"You think they dumped another body?" Ryker asked, looking around in the dark. "Why the hell else would they be out in the fields in the middle of the night?"

Colton clenched his jaw, scanning the surrounding terrain. Ryker and Jacob moved forward to investigate further, when his stomach suddenly lurched.

"Wait!" Colton yelled, rushing forward. His eyes scanned the recently disturbed earth near some of the crops.

"What do you see?" Ryker asked. "You think they rigged explosives in a damn coco field?" He grabbed his canteen and took a swig of water as he stopped.

Colton nodded. "Yep. That's exactly what I think. The farmers don't want the government eradication teams tearing out their crops," he said, kneeling down. He picked up a small pinch of dirt, rubbing it between his gloved fingertips. "This soil is really dry. They wouldn't be able to dig very deep to conceal any fresh IEDs."

"Tearing out their crops?" Jacob asked. "What the hell happened to spraying the illegal crops? That sure as hell would be a lot quicker. No wonder cocaine production is back up."

Ryker stood facing the coco fields, legs spread wide, hands on his hips. "They plant explosives to keep them from destroying the crops? Damn."

"IEDs," Colton confirmed. "It thwarts anyone attempting to remove the caco fields. It also prevents other cartels from moving in. Look over there though," he said, pointing. "You can see someone recently walked this way. Either they knew exactly where the explosives were planted or they were pretty damn lucky."

"You think it was whoever was driving that van?" Jacob asked. "Hell."

"I don't know what to think. We found that other body. I'm guessing this is another one."

Hunter's voice came over their headsets. "We've arrived at the outskirts of the warehouse where the auction was supposed to be held. Don't see a damn person here. No cars, no people, nothing. Either we're really fucking early, or the whole damn thing was called off."

"Shit," Colton muttered, anger piercing through him. Their one lead seemed to be evaporating right before their eyes. Nothing like finding out exactly where Camila was supposed to be and then having the entire operation turn to dust.

His gaze swept into the distance, where the sky still glowed orange from the SUV explosion. The helicopters had already left the area, but the remains of the blaze and whatever lights emergency crews had put up gave an eerie glow off in the distance.

A woman's scream suddenly pierced the air, and Colton's blood ran cold.

"Hell," Ryker said, taking a step forward.

"Wait," Colton said, grabbing his arm. "The IEDs. Don't go running in there."

"Hello!" Colton called out. "Is anyone there?"

"I doubt they'll answer in English," Jacob said dryly, turning around in a full circle as he scanned the surrounding area.

A woman called out in Spanish, her words much too rapid for Colton to understand a single thing. Her voice sounded weak. Tired. A brief twist of grief in his gut had something in his brain flickering in recognition and adrenaline suddenly rushing through his veins. He took a breath of the cool, crisp air. Gazed directly into the dark fields. "Camila!" he shouted.

"You think that's her?" Ryker asked in disbelief.

"Don't go in there," Jacob warned. "You said yourself IEDs were planted all over it."

"Then who better to find her than a damn explosives expert," Colton muttered. "The trampled path might have fresh IEDs that they buried on the way out. Or they might have been in too much of a rush to do anything. But if I avoid the rest of the rows of caco, I should be able to see any threats."

"Hell of a way to harvest their crops," Ryker

muttered. "I never heard of blowing up your own damn fields."

"Camila!" Colton shouted again, warmth rushing through his chest. He waited impatiently, silent enough to hear a pin drop. The second she answered he was moving in. Finding her. Consequences be damned.

"Help me," a thin voice called out.

"Cover me," Colton said, eyeing his other teammates. "I'm gonna go get my girl."

Chapter 14

Camila shivered in the night air, curled into a ball on the cold earth. Her wrists ached from where they were bound together, and her muscles were stiff from lying on the ground for so long. She had to be dreaming. Because somewhere in the distance, she could have sworn she'd heard Colton calling out her name.

Colton.

The man she'd slept with in Miami. The man who'd had her begging and pleading and then left the next morning as they'd each taken a different flight.

They'd parted ways sated and satisfied. Content to never see one another again.

Except she'd thought of him every day since.

Maybe she was hallucinating. When she hadn't been aware, her kidnappers had probably slipped her some other type of drug to make her complacent. To make sure she didn't wander off before their return.

Because there was no way on earth the man she'd

had a one-night-stand with a few weeks ago was down here in Colombia, searching for her in a dark caco field.

There was no way someone like him would be looking for her.

"Camila," that deep voice said again. "Where are you, kitten?"

Tears pricked her eyes, and her heart begin to flutter. What an unfair dream to have, when she knew in reality her kidnappers would be back. That she'd never be free again. She whimpered on the ground, shivering. Closed her eyes tightly and willed this all to be over soon. Begged God that she'd somehow be free.

A dark silhouette suddenly loomed over her, and she was too scared to even scream. Too disoriented to understand.

A man knelt down beside her dressed in camo fatigues, helmet, and some sort of night-vision goggles. A weapon was clutched tightly in his gloved hands. Large combat boots covered his feet.

Before she could even scream he was soothing her, collecting her into his muscular arms. A familiar scent washed over her, and she began sobbing, knowing now that it really was just a dream.

Gently he stood, cradling her to him. Breathing a sigh of relief.

"I'm here, kitten," Colton said. "I'm taking you home with me."

Chapter 15

Colton's gaze swept over the woman sleeping beside him. She'd been so out of it when they found her, he wasn't even sure if she realized this was all real. Her dark hair cascaded over the seats across from him where she lay curled up, a Navy-issued blanket draped over her. Although she had some scrapes and bruises, he wasn't sure what, if any, other injuries she'd sustained. She'd go straight to the hospital when they landed; ambulances were already on standby.

And hell if he wouldn't have a lot of explaining to do.

Hunter walked over to him, eyeing him carefully. "I just spoke with the CO. We can get her a refugee visa to temporarily stay in the U.S. If she agrees to cooperate with the authorities and provide whatever intel she can, that'll make the process much smoother."

"Hell," Colton said, scrubbing a hand over his face. "This is a damn lot to take in. I was so focused on rescuing her, I didn't even think about the loopholes we'd have to jump through when we got home."

"It was easier for Emma," Hunter said. "With her background in archeology, it was no problem getting her a work visa and green card to stay here in the U.S."

"Yeah," Colton said bitterly. "I guess it's not exactly the same when your father is head of a notorious drug cartel."

"Nope," Hunter agreed. "It doesn't mean something can't be worked out though if she wants to stay."

Colton chuffed out a laugh. "If? Hell, she was kidnapped by her own bodyguards. You think she'd want to go back to that life?"

"Don't know. But I'm guessing you'll have a lot of explaining to do when she wakes up."

Colton's gaze slid back to Camila. "Ain't that the truth. Hopefully she won't be pissed as hell at me for not telling her who I was back in Miami. Rescuing her has to count for something, right?"

Hunter looked over to Camila's sleeping form. "One thing I know? Don't count on anything for sure with women. She may think you're her savior, or she may be mad as hell."

"Wonderful," Colton quipped.

Ryker strode down the middle of the aisle of the C-17. "Did you see that message from the CO? Analysts are already going over the data we collected from the laptop. The operation may have gone to hell with Miguel being taken out, but we retrieved a hell of a lot of information."

Colton's gaze slid over the pale features on

Camila's normally caramel-colored skin. She had dark circles under her eyes, and her face was wan. She looked so damn innocent sleeping across from him. He'd helped her into a spare pair of fatigues before they'd gotten onto the plane. The large clothing had swallowed her much smaller, curvy frame, and she'd been so disoriented, he wasn't sure she even realized who he was or what had happened.

He'd do damn near everything in his power to make it right though. Explain to her about Miami. Tell her who he was and what he did. Not every career involved flying off to foreign countries and tracking down armed men. She had to realize he was U.S. military.

That didn't mean she'd be happy about it though.

An hour into their flight she stirred, crying out as she awoke from her sleep. Colton was at her side in an instant, crouching down beside her. "Shhh, kitten," he whispered. "I'm here."

Ryker snickered from a few seats over, and Colton shot him a look that could kill.

Chocolate brown eyes opened to meet his concerned gaze. "Colton?" she asked, her voice weak. "What's going on?"

He cleared his throat. "You're on a flight back to the U.S. We'll get you to a hospital to get checked out as soon as you arrive. I know you're dehydrated and may have other injuries." His chest tightened as his eyes ran over her. Camila was here. Alive. Whatever she'd dealt with he'd help her to face. If she wanted him.

"Are you hurt anywhere, kitten?" he asked softly.

"Just some scrapes and bruises," she said.

"They didn't—hurt you?" He didn't move a

muscle, eyeing her carefully. Not knowing what had happened to her was almost worse than knowing the truth. Worst-case scenarios were tumbling through his mind. She hadn't been missing for long, but any number of men could have taken advantage of her. Hurt her.

"They were planning to sell me at an auction," she whispered. "Some type of sex-trafficking ring like the type my father was involved in." Her voice became choked, and tears started running down her cheeks. Her body trembled, and without thinking, Colton moved closer, pulling her into his arms.

She shuddered against him, quietly sobbing, and Colton felt his chest tighten in anguish. His arms tightened around her.

"You're U.S. military," she whispered after a few minutes.

"That's right," he agreed, wiping a tear from her cheek as she pulled away and straightened. Her tearful gaze slid around the plane.

"What are you? Some type of military commandos?"

"Navy SEALs," he confirmed. "We were sent down to Colombia to track down your father."

Camila gasped, pulling away from him. "You knew who I was," she accused. "When we were in Miami, you knew exactly who I was."

Colton eyed her with a level gaze, deciding the truth was the only thing worth saying at this point. "That's right. We knew you were Miguel Rodriguez's daughter."

"So you what?" she asked, a hurt look on her face. "Targeted me? Came after me? I didn't have any information on my father—I still don't."

"We know," he said gently. "You're not in any sort of trouble."

"But you used me!" she said, fresh tears rolling down her cheeks. "You found me in the airport and took me to bed. What did you do? Go through all of my belongings when I was finally asleep?"

Colton's silence was apparently all the answer that she needed.

"Kitten," he hedged.

"Don't call me kitten!" she snapped. Reaching out, she tried to push him away. "Isn't there someone else here I can speak to? I'm done listening to your lies."

"Camila—"

"No! You took advantage of the situation. You're just as bad as those other men who kidnapped me— you wanted something for yourself so you just reached out and took it!"

"I didn't force you to do anything," Colton said in a low voice.

"Force me? No. You seduced me, making me think you were interested in me as a woman. Not as the daughter of Miguel Rodriguez. Was that your plan all along? Get me into bed so you could go through my things? Go away. Just go!" she shouted.

Hunter hurried over, eyeing the two of them. "Let me talk to her, C-4," he said, calling Colton by his nickname.

"C-4?" Camila asked as Colton stood and moved back across the aisle.

"His SEAL nickname," Hunter said, kneeling down in the aisle beside Camila. "There was no one better to search though a damn caco field riddled with explosives than our own explosives expert."

Camila looked momentarily astonished and then

sank back into her seat, shutting her eyes. She trembled as Hunter began speaking in a low voice to her, and Colton felt knots forming in his stomach. Sure, he'd rescued her, but at what cost?

She wasn't wrong in her accusations that he'd used her.

He'd fucking loved every minute of her in his bed, but when push came to shove? It had happened exactly like she said. He'd wanted her for himself and taken her back to his room. Spent the night loving her body. A brief pang of regret filled his chest.

Camila began to quietly sob again, and Colton watched as Hunter stood, shooting him a look. Fucking wonderful. The woman he'd wanted was only a few feet away, and she didn't want a damn thing to do with him.

Chapter 16

Camila opened her eyes, glancing around the hospital room. An IV was taped to her arm, providing her body with much-needed fluids. The hospital gown she had on was itchy and uncomfortable, not to mention the most unflattering piece of clothing in the world. The thin blanket covering her did little to ward of the chill. She shivered slightly, her eyes roaming the stark room.

"Knock knock," a cheerful voice said.

Camila looked over, seeing a nurse in scrubs peering into the room. She had long, strawberry-blonde hair and a stethoscope around her neck.

"I'm actually one of the pediatric ER nurses," she said, walking into Camila's room.

"ER? Like the emergency room?"

"Exactly. I'm not one of your nurses, but I wanted to come up and introduce myself. I'm Alison Garrett. My fiancé Evan works with Colton over at Little Creek."

"Little Creek?"

"The Navy SEAL base nearby."

"Oh." She was baffled. Colton had sent someone here to check in on her? She'd been so exhausted, she hardly even remembered landing in the U.S. One of the other men on the plane, Hunter, had helped her down to the ambulance. Colton had watched from afar, looking like he wanted to help.

She'd refused to let him anywhere near her.

"I know there's a lot going on right now," she said, adjusting the stethoscope around her neck. Camila's eyes were drawn to the big diamond on her ring finger.

Alison saw her looking and held up her hand. "I just got engaged," she said, sounding somewhat giddy. "We had a baby boy a few months ago, so it seemed like the right time."

"Congratulations," Camila automatically replied. Her eyes ran over the petite woman. She was small and lithe—it was hard to imagine her with one of the massive guys Colton was with.

"Evan's on a different SEAL team, but we all know each other. Not many of the guys on Colton's team have girlfriends—just Hunter. You met him already. His girlfriend Emma is British and just moved here. Anyway. I work here at the hospital, so Colton asked if I'd check in on you. And if you have any questions or anything, let me know. I'll do whatever I can to make you more comfortable."

"How long will I be kept in the hospital?"

"I'm not sure," Alison admitted. "It depends on the extent of your injuries. But Hunter probably already explained that we have a temporary visa for you to stay in the U.S. Unless you're hoping to return to Colombia?"

Camila shuddered. "Aside from my friends, there's nothing for me there."

"Right. Well, it's a lot to think about, I know. You can stay with any of us while you're recovering. Evan and I have a new baby, so we may not be the best choice, although of course you'd be welcome. My best friend Rebecca is actually due any day with her little one."

"Wow. Lots of babies," she murmured.

"Yep. We like to tease the guys that they're falling like dominoes. Every guy on Evan's team actually has a wife or girlfriend. We all look out for each other. I know you don't know any of them yet, but if you ever needed help, they'd be there, no question."

Camila nodded, unsure.

"Hunter and Emma said you could stay with them," Alison continued. "Of course, I know Colton would have you in a heartbeat, but I'm not sure—"

"Absolutely not," Camila said, shaking her head. The last thing she needed was Colton around confusing her. Pretending to be interested when he only wanted information he thought that she had.

"He does care about you," Alison said softly. "I know it's not any of my business, but—"

"No, it's not any of your business. I appreciate you coming to visit me, but Colton? I'm not interested in seeing him right now."

"Right. Well, I'm just downstairs in the ER if you need anything. Sorry if I talked your ear off. I've been on maternity leave for several months. I can't tell you how great it feels to be around adults again."

Camila smiled. She'd never imagined having a normal life—a husband, a child. Hunter had said she could get a visa to stay here in the U.S., but then what?

She'd never worked before. She'd left Colombia without a single thing. Not that she begrudged the men from rescuing her—being sold in an auction would be a fate worse than death. And if she'd somehow escaped on her own?

Those men would still come for her.

Find her.

There was no one left to be trusted, aside from her closest friends. Instantly, her mind flashed back to the café where she'd left Rosa behind. What had happened to her?

She closed her eyes, listening to the machines around her. There was too much to think about. Too many complications.

The very last thing she needed was another man telling her how she should live her own life.

***

"So, you're all set," the nurse said the next afternoon. "You could stay here in the hospital another day if you needed, but Hunter sweet-talked us into letting you leave."

"Just doing my job, ma'am," Hunter insisted.

Camila watched in astonishment as the older woman blushed. Goodness.

"Let's get you home then," Hunter said, walking over to help her stand up. "Emma went out to pick up a few things—clothes, toiletries, and girly crap like that. I'm sure you'll want to go shopping yourself, but as for now? You'll be able to relax and recover without needing anything. And like I already said, you can stay with us for a few weeks and rest up. Get your bearings."

"Thank you," Camila said, smoothing out the sweatshirt and sweatpants she'd been given. It was a far cry from the designer clothes she was used to wearing, but at the moment, comfortable sounded just about right.

"We're going to need to swing by base to get you processed properly," Hunter said. "It's not exactly the usual immigration process, but these are special circumstances. You'll get your ID and papers. And then we'll go over some options after you've had a chance to recover."

"How long is my visa good for?" Camila asked.

"Ninety days. But that's just until we can get you approved to stay in the U.S. if you want. You should be able to get a permanent visa—a green card, because of your situation. The government will be interested in finding out any knowledge you can share about your father or the Rodriguez Cartel. But going back to Colombia isn't a safe option," he said in a low voice.

"I understand," she said, tears smarting her eyes.

Was she happy that she'd been rescued or sad that she'd never return? Her entire life had been flipped upside down in simply a matter of days. She barely knew which way was up at this point—not when she'd been shaken to her very core.

Her father was gone. Her belongings. Her life.

The bodyguards she'd trusted for years were her enemy. And Rosa?

"Hey," she called out to Hunter as he led her out of the hospital room.

"Is something wrong?" he asked. His hands slid

into his pockets as he turned back toward her. His tattoos showed beneath his short-sleeve tee shirt, but he otherwise looked nothing like the tattooed men who had taken her.

The men here seemed to be as good as the others were evil—save for Colton, who'd taken her to bed only to get what he wanted.

"I want to find out about a friend of mine back in Colombia. Is there a way to do it? She was with me in the café when I was kidnapped. I want to make sure she's all right."

A concerned look crossed his face. "Can I ask her name?"

"Rosa Martinez."

"I'm sorry," he said quietly.

"Sorry we can't find out about her?"

Hunter took a step closer to her, his hand resting lightly on her forearm. She looked up at him in confusion, seeing the truth written across his face. "She didn't make it," he said quietly. "She was kidnapped as well—her body was recovered."

"No," Camila said, stepping back, trembling. "No, that can't be right."

"I'm sorry," he said, his voice gruff. He looked slightly uncomfortable but didn't leave.

"How can this be happening? My father, my best friend…. It just doesn't seem fair. Everything was fine just a couple of days ago. And now?" She shrugged helplessly. What words could even begin to describe her grief, the magnitude of her loss.

She'd come here with nothing. Lost everything. And the only friend she seemed to have at the moment was the leader of a Navy SEAL team. The very same one the man she hated more than anyone in the world was on.

How convenient.

One man was trying to help her; one man used her.

She hastily scrubbed the tears from her face as other patients and hospital staff eyed her curiously in the hallway. "Let's just get out of here," she said, her voice cracking. "Let's get the papers or whatever I need and just go."

Hunter reached toward her again, his hand resting lightly at the crook of her arm as he guided her forward. She could cry later—in the privacy of her room or bed or wherever he was taking her to spend the night. She'd recover for a day or two and then get her life back in order. Find out what type of job options she had. See if she could access any of her accounts. The Colombian government might have frozen her father's assets after his death, but she had separate bank accounts. Someway, somehow, she'd get what was hers.

Then she'd find somewhere to stay. Something to do.

She was a survivor, and being thrown for a loop wasn't going to ruin her life.

They walked out of the hospital into the bright sunlight, and Camila shielded her eyes. "My SUV is right over there," Hunter said, pointing toward a large black monstrosity. What was it with boys and their toys?

Some things were the same worldwide.

He opened the passenger door and helped her climb in. "We need to quickly swing by Little Creek. I'm sure you're exhausted, but we'll get the paperwork we need and get you settled in. Emma should be back by the time we are."

"All right," she said, sinking back into the seat. She closed her eyes, enjoying the warmth of the sun coming in through the windows.

Hunter climbed into the driver's side, and the engine roared to life a moment later. "Do you need anything? Food or drink?"

"I'm fine. Let's just get this taken care of."

"Roger that," Hunter said, easily maneuvering the large vehicle out of the parking space. They drove down a highway, and a few minutes later, they were turning down a tree-lined road. Hunter flashed his military ID and spoke to the guards at the gate, giving them her name. The men guarding the entrance cleared them to drive through, and soon they were pulling into a large parking lot.

Camila climbed out of the SUV, the salty scent of the ocean hitting her instantly. "We're near the water," she said, surprised.

"Yep. We're on a Navy base. Most are close to the ocean."

"Right, I didn't think about it. I was in Miami a week or so ago. I just didn't think of Virginia as being by the ocean—but of course it's on the coast."

"Well, it's not exactly tropical like Miami," he said with a chuckle. "But it gets hot in the summer. And if you like beaches, Virginia Beach is one of the best when the weather is right. Let's head in," he said, cocking his head toward the doors. "We'll get your stuff and get out of here."

Camila looked toward the large building on base and hesitated.

"Is something wrong?" he asked.

"No. It's nothing," she muttered, finally walking

the way he'd indicated.

"Colton?" Hunter guessed.

She bristled. "He works here, too, no? Of course I wouldn't be happy about seeing him."

Hunter blew out a sigh. "That he does. And I realize that you're pissed as hell at him. But you should know, he's the one who pushed for us to move in and rescue you. We didn't have authorization to go after you. We didn't have a reason to in the eyes of the U.S. government. Our mission was to get your father and get out. Colton was the one who made sure you were safe."

"He was?"

"Yep," Hunter said, pulling open one of the doors to base. "We were sent there on a different op. It's no secret that the U.S. and Colombian governments were both interested in your father. We planned to bring him in and question him."

"But he was killed instead."

"Not by us," Hunter assured her. "But Miguel Rodriguez was a very dangerous man. Running drugs and women doesn't exactly get you a lot of friends."

"No, it doesn't," she agreed. "My own bodyguards turned against me."

"Let's go in here," Hunter said, ushering her into a front office. "We were lucky that we got someone from State to swing by and push this through."

"What state?"

Hunter chuckled. "Sorry. One thing about the Navy? We've got loads of acronyms and shorthand terms for every government agency. The State Department handles passports, visas, immigration, and the like. This isn't exactly typical procedure—but like I said, this isn't a typical situation either. Luckily, they were willing to come to us to get you processed after your release from the hospital. When you're up for it, I'm sure they'll have some questions."

"Of course."

"Good morning," a woman in a sleek suit said, rising up from one of the chairs in the waiting area as they walked in.

Camila glanced down at her own baggy sweatpants. She hadn't even had a proper shower yet—just a quick sponge bath when she was getting cleaned up in the hospital. She looked and felt horrible. At least her clothing concealed some of her bumps and bruises, but nothing could hide the dark circles under her eyes. Or the bone deep ache she had inside.

"I know you've been through a lot," the woman said after she'd introduced herself. "Let's make this quick and painless, and you can get home to rest."

"Great. Just let me know what I need to do."

The woman guided them over to a table, and Camila sat down, signing a few papers. She was taken into a separate room and got a horrible photograph taken for her temporary ID. She cringed as she looked at it, and Hunter chuckled.

"What's so funny?" she asked sourly.

"Women are all the same." He raised an eyebrow, daring her to challenge him. "You've been through hell, and you're concerned about a picture?"

She shrugged. "I'm the one who has to look at it all the time."

Hunter held his hands up. "All right, I know when I'm beat. Emma would probably say the same thing. And you'll meet her soon. Let me just wrap a few things up, and we'll head on out."

"Okay," Camila said, sinking down into the chair. She was completely and utterly exhausted, and at the moment, she wanted nothing more than to curl up in bed and sleep for a few days. She didn't even care that she'd be staying with Hunter and his girlfriend. Anything was better than being dragged from place to place with no end in sight.

With no hope of escape.

The door to the office opened a moment later, and her eyes swept up to see Colton standing there. Shock shot straight through her, and she stood up from her seat, backing away. Glancing around the office, she saw a woman typing at a computer, but Hunter was nowhere to be found.

Damn it.

"Camila," Colton said, his voice rough. He was dressed in camouflage fatigues, his dark eyes focused on her, looking rough and ready to take on the entire world. He took a step toward her, his combat boots loud despite the carpeted floor, and she shot him an accusing look.

"I told you I didn't want to see you," she said.

"I understand. I know you're upset about what happened, and I can't change that. I sure as hell can't fix it right now," he said, glancing around. "I'm sorry for the way everything happened, but I just wanted to give this to you."

She looked suspiciously at his outstretched hand, a cell phone resting in his palm.

"Take it," he said. "It's for you."

"You got me a phone?"

"I wanted you to have a way to get help if you needed it. I know that you're frightened—hell, I don't blame you. My involvement when we met in Miami didn't exactly help matters either. I want you to trust me. My number is programmed in there, as is the rest of the team's numbers. If you need anything, I want you to call me. No questions asked—I'm there."

"I can't accept this," she said. Despite her protest, a strange warmth was spreading through her. She'd practically told the man that she hated him, and he'd gone out and gotten her a cell phone of all things.

Colton was worried about her. Wanted to keep her safe. Hunter had said himself that Colton was the one who'd insisted they find her.

Slowly she reached out, and he met her gaze, his eyes asking for forgiveness. "I want you to feel safe, kitten," he said quietly. "Go ahead and take it."

Tears smarted her eyes, and he reached out for her.

"Don't," she said, swatting his hand away.

"Keep the phone," he said. "Even if you don't need to use it, it'll make me feel better knowing that you have it. Knowing that you have a way to reach me or the team if you need to."

She nodded uncertainly, glancing up as Hunter walked back over. Colton reached into his pocket, pulling out the charger. "You'll need this, too," he said, his fingers brushing against hers as she took it from him. She tried not to tremble at his touch and took a step closer to Hunter.

Hunter had a girlfriend. He was safe. Not someone who'd try to use her just to get what he wanted.

He'd helped her without asking for anything. Stepped in when she'd made it clear she didn't want Colton visiting her in the hospital.

"Ready to go?" Hunter asked, glancing between

them. "Or do you two need a few minutes?"

Colton eyed her, waiting for her to respond.

"I'm ready to go," she said hesitantly. "But I'll take this."

Colton nodded, stepping aside to let them out the door. Camila felt conflicted as they passed him, her gut twisting. She could never give a man like that her heart, she rationalized. Not when she couldn't trust him. Not when he'd used her.

Why did her chest ache so much then when she walked out the door?

Chapter 17

Colton muttered a curse as Hunter and Camila left, leaving him standing alone in the front office. Hell of a way to welcome her to the U.S.—by sending her to live with his teammate.

What the hell did he expect?

It's not like she'd fall into his arms and bed after she realized what had happened in Miami. Sure, he'd rescued her down in Bogota—he'd never regret that. If anything, it killed him that there were other women out there missing. Helpless.

But Camila?

Helpless was the last word he'd ever use to describe her. Maybe they'd get back on good terms— eventually. It was possible she wouldn't even stay near Little Creek though. It was a damn big country. Maybe she wouldn't move back to Colombia after everything that had happened, but Miami? The west coast? There were a hell of a lot of options that didn't involve living anywhere near him.

He shoved open the door to the office and stalked down the hall to the locker room. Maybe an hour or so of lifting weights would help clear his head. At least give him something to focus on aside from her.

He jogged down a set of steps and turned the corner and spotted the Alpha SEAL team coming into the building, gear in hand, just back from their deployment to the Middle East. He nodded at Patrick, the leader of the Alpha SEALs, and Evan "Flip" Jenkins, who was walking beside him.

"Ice," he said as the other team's leader came to a stop in front of him. "Good to see you guys are back."

"Heard you just made it back from Bogota," Patrick said, dropping his heavy duffle bag to the ground. He looked tired but happy as hell to be home. And who wouldn't be in his position? He had a wife, couple of kids, and new baby on the way any day now.

"Affirmative. We didn't get Miguel but ended up with his daughter instead."

Patrick's cool blue eyes gazed at him. "I heard. Look, we've dealt with all kinds of crazy kidnapping situations between the men on our team and their girlfriends. If your woman needs anyone to talk to, let me know. I can connect her with one of the other wives or girlfriends."

Colton resisted the urge to groan. "She's not my woman. Hell, she's staying with Hunter and Emma because she won't even talk to me."

"Been there, done that," Patrick assured him with a chuckle. "Seriously. If Camila needs anything, give me a call. Rebecca and the others will be more than happy to chat with her. Well, maybe not Rebecca since the baby is due any minute. But Lexi, Ella," he said, naming the girlfriends of some of his SEAL team members. "They'd be more than happy to help."

Both women had been kidnapped in different situations. Lexi when she was tracking down hackers attempting to infiltrate Little Creek's Top Secret databases, and Ella when she'd worked as a cocktail waitress down in Florida.

It was almost damn hard to believe the amount of trouble the Alpha team had been through if Colton hadn't witnessed some of it with his own eyes. He hadn't been here at Little Creek when Lexi was taken, but when Ella was still in Florida, Colton had been stationed in Pensacola. Some of the guys on the Alpha team had come down, and when it turned out that Brent "Cobra" Rollins had a thing for Ella, he'd come down to bring her back to Virginia with him, never knowing she'd been kidnapped by some men her sleazy boss had dealt with.

There was never a dull moment with either of the SEAL teams.

Evan cleared his throat. "Maybe you didn't know, but Ali works at the hospital where Camila was taken when you arrived in the U.S. I only chatted with Ali briefly while we were gone, but she went to check in on Camila when she was there."

Colton nodded. "I appreciate it. She'll need some friends here to lean on if she decides to stay." He eyed all the gear they were hauling in. "Get going. I'm sure you're both ready to get home to your wives and kids. Girlfriend, I mean," he said, glancing back at Evan.

"Fiancée," Evan said with a grin.

"No way!" Colton said, clapping him on the back.

"Congrats man. Another one bites the dust, huh?"

Patrick chuckled. "Hoorah. Some of the guys were giving Evan a tough time on the flight back, but hell, you know we wouldn't have it any other way." He said goodbye before turning and walking away, no doubt eager to get home. Evan grabbed his buzzing cell phone from his pocket, talking quietly to Alison as he also left, and Colton was left standing there alone in the hall as the other men moved on to go about their lives.

He pushed open the door and walked into the locker room, changing from his fatigues into his PT gear. An incoming text on his phone had him doing a double take.

Camila's a mess. I give it 24 hours before she's calling you.

Colton thumbed a response to Hunter.

Is she okay?

His phone beeped with Hunter's reply a moment later.

She's scared of her own shadow. Can't say that I blame her after what she's been through.

Colton muttered a curse. He pressed the "call" button beside Hunter's name on his phone.

"Hell man, is she all right?" Colton asked. "What do you need me to do?"

Hunter cleared his throat. "It's tough to say. She burst into tears as soon as Emma gave her some clothes. Maybe she's overtired and overwhelmed from it all. I'm just saying—she'll probably be more comfortable around you than Emma and myself."

Colton felt his chest tighten. Damn it. Should he go to her? He was trying to give her space. She'd been mad as hell on the flight back to the States. The last thing she needed was another man pushing his way into her life—not that he hadn't already done exactly that down in Miami.

"Call me if I should come over," Colton instructed. "I'd like to give her a little space, but hell. If she's upset and needs someone, you know I'll be on my way."

"Roger that," Hunter said.

The two men said their goodbyes, and Colton slammed his locker door shut before stalking off to lift. If she needed him, he could be there in minutes. There was no sense in upsetting her more than she already was though by showing up unannounced on her doorstep.

Making more of a mess of the situation

It was amazing how something so simple could be so fucking complicated at the same time.

***

Camila glanced around the spare bedroom, taking in the bags of clothes Emma had purchased for her. They were piled atop the floral bedspread, but aside from a dresser and nightstand, the room was relatively bare.

"I hope you'll be able to use some of this," Emma said in her British accent, brushing a strand of red hair back behind her ear. With her pale skin and green eyes, she was as opposite in looks from Camila as one could be. She moved around the room with practiced efficiency, sorting what she'd bought and carrying another bag into the bathroom.

"Toiletries are in there," Emma said, pointing to the counter. "There are spare towels for you to use as well if you'd like a nice long bath." Camila watched her mouth in fascination as she pronounced the word. Camila had an accent as well of course when she spoke English. It was amazing how the same language could sound so very different depending on who was talking.

"Thank you," Camila said, suddenly feeling overwhelmed.

She had literally nothing to her name at the moment. No clothes. No money she could access. No home.

"I'm used to traveling light for archeological digs," Emma said. "I don't do as much of that anymore of course. Hunter said you're used to a quite different lifestyle. As soon as everything is sorted, I'm sure you'd like to purchase your own things. This is just to tide you over."

"I don't have anything right now, so this is perfect," Camila assured her. "I need something to wear, no?"

"That's absolutely right," Emma said. "So, let me know if you need anything else. We can pick up some foods you like at the market—grocery store," she amended. "But if you'd like a nice cup of tea now or biscuits, let me know."

"Biscuits?" Camila asked in confusion.

"Cookies," Hunter said from the door with a chuckle. He took a step into the room, taking a swig of the beer he was holding. For some reason it reminded her of Colton, and tears smarted her eyes. She was intruding on Hunter and Emma's life—a stranger with nothing to her name at the moment. It seemed that they'd just gotten this house together. And now she was barging in because she had nowhere to go.

"Everything all right?" Hunter asked.

"I think she just needs a moment," Emma assured him, walking over and taking his hand. Hunter towered above her petite frame, and Camila watched as they walked away. Hunter pulled out his phone to text someone, and Camila's gaze fell on the phone sitting on the nightstand.

Colton was just a phone call away if she needed him. Not that she needed a man in her life, but despite her anger toward Colton, she still felt like he'd protect her if she needed him. He'd protect her life, she thought as she considered it. He didn't seem to have any reservations about trampling right over her heart though.

Chapter 18

Emma dropped Camila off down by the beach a few days later before heading into work. "Are you sure you'll be all right to walk around alone for a few hours?" she asked in her smooth British accent. "I can work from home again," she assured her.

Camila glanced into the backseat at the pile of books and papers Emma had. The poor woman had done enough over the past few days while Camila rested. She needed to get out and get some fresh air as much as Emma needed to get on with her own life.

"I'll be fine," Camila assured her.

"All right," Emma finally said, looking over her from head to toe. "I'll meet you here in a couple of hours on my lunch break and bring you back home. Call me if you need anything—anything at all," she stressed. "Hunter and the guys are on base, but they could get here too if you're in trouble."

After saying goodbye, Camila's heart pounded slightly more than she wanted to admit as she watched Emma's car drive off down the block. It was silly of her to feel skittish to walk around the crowded boardwalk area. She'd traveled alone in the past. She'd loved her weekends away in Miami. Just because her father's men had turned on her didn't mean she was in danger wherever she went.

Not everyone in the world was after her.

She turned back toward the beach, gazing up the long boardwalk that ran up and down the strip. Although it was the beginning of spring in Colombia, it was a warm fall afternoon in the northern hemisphere. Odd how the world was so different depending on which part of it you were in, Camila mused. Virginia Beach was nothing like Bogota or even the fast-paced Miami, where she loved to visit. There was something oddly calming about the families and locals wandering around the beach though. Presumably the summer months were filled with tourists, but right now it was relatively quiet and serene.

She walked along the boardwalk, enjoying the views of the ocean and the feel of the salty air whipping through her hair. The long sundress Emma had bought for her blew gently in the ocean breeze. It wasn't exactly her usual style of clothing. She preferred trendy, short, and sexy—high heels, make-up, the whole nine yards.

Camila had trashed the flirty little dress she'd been kidnapped in though, right along with her designer heeled sandals. Never seeing either of those items again would be too soon.

Her dark hair blew in the breeze, and she clutched the strong cup of coffee they'd picked up on the way over in her hand. Emma had a large assortment of teas at the house, but it wasn't nearly strong enough for Camila given how little shut eye she'd gotten the past few nights.

Her sleep last night had been fitful, filled with tossing and turning and nightmares. She'd awoken more than once in a cold sweat, tempted to call Colton. Trembling as she tossed and turned under the covers wasn't going to get her any rest.

She needed to stand up for herself though— survive on her own.

She didn't doubt he would've come if she'd called him, but then what? She still had an entire new life to forge for herself. She didn't exactly trust him enough to confide in him or ask him for help starting over. Not unless her situation was life or death.

Her cell phone buzzed with an incoming text, and she scanned Hunter's message in surprise.

Sounds like you'll be able to access your accounts soon. Luckily some of the guys on base have friends in high places.

Camila let out a sigh of relief. Even if she didn't have a cent to her name at the moment, she knew that Hunter and his SEAL team could help her get it sorted. They'd stormed into Colombia and rescued her in the middle of a field, hadn't they? The fact that she'd agreed to meet with Pentagon officials providing as much information as she could about her father's operations certainly helped smooth things over, she was sure.

She didn't know much, but they appeared interested in any small detail she could provide.

The hotels became fewer and farther between the more she walked down the boardwalk. The busy strip eventually gave way to beachfront homes when the boardwalk ended. She glanced around, slightly worried, and realized she should have been paying closer attention when Emma dropped her off earlier. It was blocks and blocks from where she was supposed to meet her for lunch. Even if she hurried back right now, she'd probably be late.

And there was no doubt Emma would be worried.

A cool breeze began to blow in from the ocean as she turned around, and she noticed some storm clouds rolling in from the distance.

Perfect.

She didn't have a coat or umbrella and was nowhere close to where she was supposed to be.

She tossed her empty coffee cup into a trashcan just as a few drops of rain began to fall. They sprinkled down on her cheeks and hair as she glanced skyward, and before long, fat water droplets were coming down. She looked around in disdain, realizing there was no way to avoid being completely soaked.

"Hey there!" a guy walking his dog called out as she passed a large hotel. "Can you give me directions to Seafare? I'm running late."

She eyed him warily, shaking her head "no."

He was just someone turned around like her, she reassured herself. A person asking her for directions didn't mean anything was wrong. Or that someone was after her. The beach and boardwalk began to clear of people as the rain steadily fell, and she started walking faster, the cool rain beginning to chill her bare skin.

Panic began to set in as she saw two men in the distance jogging toward her. They were muscular and fit, seeming unfazed to be out running in the pouring rain. Her heart began to pound, and she took a deep breath, trying to calm down. She was on a public beach with hotels and restaurants all around. She could run to any of them if she needed help. Her paranoia was only due to the events of the past week.

The cold rain began to soak through her sundress, and to her astonishment, she realized it had become nearly see-through now that it was wet. The pink lacy bra she'd put on showed right through the dress, and the two men jogging eyed her appreciatively as they approached.

Normally she relished attention of that sort, but right now?

She wished she could curl up into a little ball and disappear. There was nothing appealing about being vulnerable in a strange city—not after what had happened only days before.

"Hey there, beautiful!" one of the men who'd jogged by called out as he turned back around, heading over to her.

"I'm not interested," she muttered, walking back toward the busier part of the strip.

"Do you need to get out of the rain?" he asked. "We've got a couple of hotel rooms a block over." His gaze fell to her chest, and heated embarrassment washed over her.

"I'm not interested," she repeated, picking up her pace.

"Hey beautiful, don't be like that," he said, lightly touching her arm.

She screamed and jumped away from him, watching as he backed away in surprise. "Chill out, lady," he said.

She trembled, taking another step away from him, and then turned and ran. She didn't even care where she was headed, as long as it was far away from both of them. Racing toward the first covered area she spotted, she ran into a large parking garage attached to a luxury hotel. She didn't want to rush into the lobby and make a scene, soaking wet and panicked, but the garage would shelter her from the rain at least while she called Emma.

Rubbing her damp fingers on her soggy dress as she tried to dry them, she swiped the screen on the phone Colton had given her with a trembling hand. Hunter's name was right at the top as her most recent contact, with Emma's right below.

She glanced up as a car pulled into the garage, its headlights cutting through the dim light. Hesitating only a second, she scrolled down to Colton's name.

She froze as she listened to it ring on the other end of the line, debating if she should just hang up altogether. She hadn't even spoken to him for a few days, when she'd made it clear he'd betrayed her. Her heart pounded in her chest, and just as she almost lost her nerve, Colton answered, his deep voice ricocheting right through her. Doing funny things to her insides. Making her feel warm and safe despite the chill.

"Kitten, are you okay?" he asked. "Hunter said Emma was looking for you. You were supposed to meet up for lunch? Where are you?"

"There were these guys," she gasped, choking back a sob. "I was on the boardwalk, in the rain. I was walking—" she cut off, taking a deep breath, realizing she wasn't making any sense.

"What guys?" Colton asked, immediately sounding alert. "Are you okay?"

"They just—they were following me. They wanted me to come back to their hotel to get out of the rain.

He touched my arm, and I panicked. Now I'm soaking wet in a parking garage somewhere—I don't even know where I am. What if they come back?"

"I'll come get you," he said immediately. "Are you right by the beach? Did they follow you?"

"No, I got scared and ran away. I'm in a parking garage," she repeated, looking around as she wiped her eyes. "I ran in here to get out of the rain. I'm not sure where exactly—I think it's attached to a hotel. I walked and walked after Emma dropped me off—the boardwalk ended, and there were just houses." Unable to stop herself, she burst into tears.

"Kitten, what's the name of the hotel? Are you at the north end of the beach?"

"I don't know," she gasped, taking in big gulps of air. "I can go look, I guess. I'm scared. I just don't know what to do."

"I'll ping your phone," Colton said.

"What do you mean?" she asked, taking another deep breath.

"Track your location. We've got computer guys on base—should take just a minute or two. I'll be there in twenty minutes"

"But why?"

"Why what?"

"Why are you willing to come? I told you the other day that I didn't even want to talk to you, no? And now you're willing to drop everything and come find me?"

There was a pause on the other end of the line. "I want you to be safe, kitten. Hell, if you don't want to stay with me, I'll drive you back to Hunter and Emma's. Drop you off at another team member's house. Wherever you want to go. Wherever you'd feel safe. But I'm not about to leave you alone and scared."

"Okay," she whispered, looking around as a car engine started. "Please hurry."

That seemed to snap Colton back to attention, because suddenly he was all business again. "I'm on my way, kitten. Don't move. I'm coming to get you."

Chapter 19

Colton flew down Atlantic Avenue, the road that ran parallel to the Virginia Beach strip, white knuckling the steering wheel of his SUV. Fucking hell. What on earth had made Emma think it was all right to leave Camila alone in a strange city? In a foreign country?

After all that she'd been through, Colton knew she was hanging on by a thread.

He pulled to a stop at a red light, the windshield wipers on his SUV swishing quickly back and forth. Hell. He was warm and safe in his car, able to go wherever he wanted.

But Camila?

She'd been stuck out in the rain, lost and scared. She'd been scared since she first got to the U.S. Maybe she didn't want to admit it, but he'd seen it in her eyes when they'd been on base. She was mad that he'd played her, sure. But she was also scared out of her mind.

Colton had rushed over to one of his buddies in

IT at Little Creek half an hour ago when she called and gotten them to track the GPS on the phone he'd given Camila. Ironic that as pissed as she'd been after Miami, it was the fact that he'd given her a phone that allowed him to track her down today. He could've found her eventually. He'd have driven to every damn garage up and down Atlantic Avenue if she needed him.

Briefly, he wondered about all of her belongings left in Colombia. If someone else from one of the cartels ended up with them, they'd possibly be able to track some of the other members that way. He'd have to get with some of the IT staff to make sure that was happening. Sure, the original plan was to go after Miguel, but if the surveillance equipment was in place, they might as well take full advantage of it. After everything he and Camila had been through together, he didn't want the fact that he'd bugged her belongings to be in vain.

Pulling his SUV to a stop just inside the garage, he jumped out and scanned the area. His eyes tracked over the parked vehicles, stairwells, and dim lights, and he finally spotted Camila huddled over by the stairwell in the corner. Another door there led to the street, but she was mostly hidden from view.

"Camila," he called out in a low voice, not wanting to frighten her.

She looked up at him with wet eyes, and he saw that she was trembling. "Fucking hell," he muttered to himself, rushing over. He was tugging off his camo jacket in an instant, draping it over her slender shoulders as he crouched down in front of her. The long sundress she had on was soaked through, and she was shivering from the cold. He clenched his jaw as he saw the outline of her lacy bra beneath it—no wonder those jackasses on the boardwalk were chasing after her.

"Kitten," he said gruffly, pulling her into his embrace. Letting her slender body relax into his own. "Are you okay? Tell me that you're all right."

"I'm fine," she said, burying her head in her hands. Shaking as he cradled her against his chest.

He ran a hand over her wet hair. "You're not fine, but I'm going to make sure you're okay. And I'm pissed as hell at Hunter and Emma for thinking it was okay to drop you off at the beach for the morning."

"I just want to get out of here," she said, glancing up at him.

Her chocolate brown eyes were filled with anguish, and his heart clenched. "I'll take you home, kitten. Back to Hunter's. Wherever you need to go to feel safe."

"You risked your life to save me," she whispered. "Back in Colombia—you could have been killed walking through those fields. Hunter told me all about how dangerous it was—how you insisted the team couldn't leave until you rescued me."

"Hell, kitten, I'd walk through fires to make sure that you're all right."

"But we barely even know each other. We spent one night together and parted."

He met her gaze, taking one of her hands into his much larger one. "We know each other. I know how it feels when I'm kissing you for hours. When our bodies are joined together, and I can't tell where I end and you begin. I know what it sounds like when you're calling out my name, your body clenching down around my cock. I've known you since I spotted you arguing with the TSA agents in Miami about your moisturizer."

"Facial cleanser," she said with a small laugh.

"Hell, whatever it was, you were mine from the moment I took your bag at the airport and talked you into getting a drink. That spark in your eye, that sexy laugh, and flirtatious voice. Your goddamn red lipstick all over my body."

He shuddered as she smiled at him. "I need to buy more—I have nothing here."

"We'll get it. Anything. And as for everything else there is to learn about one another? We'll take our time. Whether that's at my place, Hunter and Emma's, or a place you get on your own, I'm in no hurry. Whatever you need to be comfortable and safe here."

"I want to stay with you," she admitted.

"You want to come live with me?" he murmured softly, brushing a wet lock of her hair back from her face.

"Yes," she whispered. "I feel safe when you're with me. I can't explain it—I'm still mad about what happened, how you went looking for me intentionally in the airport, but my heart? My heart can't resist how I feel when we're together."

Fresh tears began streaming down her face, and Colton thumbed them away.

"Hell, kitten. You've had my heart since the moment we met. Let's get you home."

"To your home," she clarified.

"To our home."

***

Camila walked out of the master bedroom in Colton's townhouse, padding out into the living room. She had on one of his large tee shirts, with Emma promising to drop off her few belongings later that night.

Colton crossed the room to her, taking her hand in his. "You smell like me," he said huskily, ducking down and kissing the top of her head. "My shampoo. My body wash."

"I don't have any of my things."

"I know. And there's something sexy as fuck about seeing you wearing my tee shirt and nothing else."

"I don't know," she teased, playfully turning away. "Wearing nothing at all might be sexier, no?"

"Camila," he chided, watching with heated eyes as her fingers playfully trailed over the hem of the tee shirt she had on. It hit at mid-thigh, but she was slowly pulling it up, watching him in amusement. "Kitten, I'd take you to bed in an instant. But don't you need to rest after the past week?"

She paused, her eyes roaming over his body. In a tee shirt and his camo fatigues, his muscled body was displayed to perfection. She couldn't ignore the impressive bulge at the front of his pants. "Why, do you have something you need to do? Get back to base perhaps, and leave me here all alone?"

She tugged the tee shirt up and over her head and was standing before him naked. His gaze fell to her full breasts, heating her from within. She still had a few scrapes and fading bruises on her arms and legs, but for the first time since she'd been kidnapped, she felt like herself again. Sexy. Free. Addicted to the man before her.

Colton crossed over to her, lifting her up into his

muscular arms.

"Kitten, did they hurt you? Because I don't want to do anything that would cause you any pain."

"I'm fine, lover," she murmured. "They didn't do anything like what you're thinking."

"Thank God," he muttered, briefly resting his forehead against hers. Her arms wound around his neck, and then Colton was carrying her into his bedroom. Kissing her. Lying her down on his bed.

He stripped off his own shirt, and her gaze raked over him—broad shoulders, sculpted pecs, and a chiseled abdomen that looked to be carved from granite. A beat later he was coming down on top of her. Kissing her softly as his hands landed on either side of her head. Boxing her in with his muscled arms. Making her feel safe.

His lips moved against hers, his tongue seeking entrance, and she gasped and opened to him, letting Colton take complete control. As she lay gasping for breath, he began moving down her body. Teeth grazed her neck, sending shivers racing down her spine. His tongue swiped where he'd nipped at her, and he kissed his way lower. One large hand palmed and kneaded one breast, claiming what was his. His thumb moved over her nipple, rubbing back and forth, teasing her until she was whimpering for more.

His mouth moved to her other breast, and he kissed his way around one nipple, leaving her gasping at the sensations shooting through her. Finally, his tongue found her taut bud, licking it slowly as she whimpered. He gently flicked his tongue back and forth, driving her wild, and then finally his teeth grazed over her nipple as she squealed, her pussy flooding with arousal.

Colton kissed his way down her stomach, and then he was parting her thighs with his hands, opening her fully to him. He didn't tease her like their night in Miami, just dove straight in, like he could never possibly have enough of her.

His broad shoulders spread her legs wide for him, leaving her sex vulnerable and open, and then she was at his complete and utter mercy. His lips kissed and caressed her folds, leaving her whimpering and gasping for more. With a few hard swipes of his tongue, she was crying out, nearing the precipice. Two thick fingers sank into her molten channel, and then his tongue lightly traced circles around her clit as she cried out on his bed.

Her fingernails raked through his cropped hair as his fingers pumped in and out of her core.

She moaned before him, not knowing whether she wanted to beg him to stop or demand he continue. His tongue laved over her throbbing clit again, and then he sucked it into his mouth as she screamed.

Pulses of white-hot arousal flashed through her, sending her impossibly higher and higher as her orgasm went on and on. As she lay gasping for breath on his bed, Colton stepped out of his pants and boxers and sheathed his throbbing cock. It jutted skyward, ready and eager for her, and in a moment, he was hovering over her body, slowly pushing inside.

She murmured at the intimate invasion, as he gently stroked her inner walls with his thick length. Colton finally bottomed out, the base of his erection rubbing up against her still-throbbing clit. Slowly, he began to thrust in and out, trapping her in his heated gaze. She gasped with each deep stroke, and he ducked down and kissed her softly, before his tongue traced the seam of her lips.

He swallowed her cries as he began to thrust faster. Harder.

Impossibly, she felt herself being built up again. Her legs wrapped around his hips, and sparks of pleasure began to race through her body. Each deep thrust sent her closer to the edge as Colton claimed her again and again, until finally her inner walls clamped down around him and she cried out his name.

Afterward they lay intertwined in each other's arms, Camila resting her head on Colton's strong chest.

"Stay here, kitten," he said, his fingers lazily running through her hair.

"I'm not going anywhere, lover."

"I mean stay here with me. Don't go back to Hunter's house."

"You really want me to move in with you?"

"Hell yeah, I want you to move in with me. So it's a little fast. I want you in my arms and in my bed, safe and sound."

"Yes."

"Yes, you'll move in with me?"

"*Sí.* I will move in with you. I just said this, no?"

Colton chuckled. "Yes, no, whatever you say. As long as you're moving in, I'll be a happy man. You've been mine ever since I saw you in Miami, kitten."

Camila smiled, her eyes heating. "And that's where you're wrong. Ever since Miami, you've been mine, lover." She turned in his arms, lifting herself up so that she was straddling him. His erection sprang to life, and she shamelessly rubbed herself against him, enjoying the feel of his thick length against her arousal-slickened sex. Colton let her think she was in control, and then at the last second, flipped her over beneath him as she squealed in delight. He ducked lower and kissed her, pinning her wrists above her head.

"Take me, lover," she purred, gazing up at him.

In another instant he was inside her, claiming her as his once more.

She was finally home.

Exactly where she belonged.

THE END

About the Author

Makenna Jameison is a bestselling romance author. She writes military romance and romantic suspense with hot alpha males, steamy scenes, and happily-ever-afters.

Her debut series made it to #1 in Romance Short Stories on Amazon. Makenna loves the beach, strong coffee, red wine, and traveling. She lives in Washington DC with her husband and two daughters.

Visit www.makennajameison.com to discover your next great read.

Want to read more from MAKENNA JAMEISON?

Keep reading for an exclusive excerpt from the eleventh book in her Alpha SEALs series, *RESCUED BY A SEAL.*

Navy SEAL Mason "Riptide" Ryan has been flirting with the gorgeous waitress he met at Anchors for months. The petite brunette is shy, sweet, and sexy-as-hell—exactly the type of woman he wants. Mason's ready to convince her he's playing for keeps if she'll take a risk and give him her heart.

Taylor Reynolds knows a good thing when she sees it—and the handsome, sexy, and flirty Navy SEAL meets all the marks. His strength and confidence leave her flushing every time he's near, and she'd be willing to give him a shot if her controlling ex-boyfriend didn't keep showing up at her door.

When her ex decides he's not willing to let Taylor go without a fight, Mason is the only man who can rescue her. But will the assertive Navy SEAL be able to convince Taylor that their relationship is worth fighting for, too?

RESCUED BY A SEAL, a standalone novel, is book eleven in the sizzling Alpha SEALs series.

Chapter 1

Mason "Riptide" Ryan jumped and shot the basketball from the three-point line, listening to the "swoosh" of the ball as it sunk into the net after sailing through the air. He smoothly landed back on the blacktop and swiped his brow with his forearm.

Nothing like an outside game of hoops on a gorgeous evening, the salty ocean air from a few blocks away blowing around them.

"Whoo-hoo, sailor!" a woman from a group hanging outside the fence of the basketball court shouted. "You can sink into me anytime!"

"Becky!" her friend admonished, shushing her.

Mason smirked as the two women walked away, sashaying in their skimpy shorts and tank tops. He and his teammates were playing on a court at the edge of base, where some of the local women were known to congregate in hopes of catching a glimpse of the Navy SEALs.

And vice versa.

Nothing wrong with playing ball with his buddies

while he had a few attractive women cheering them on.

He watched the hips of the woman who'd shouted at him temptingly sway back and forth as she and her friend moved toward a row of men jogging around the perimeter, pausing to smile and wave at the young recruits.

Her short shorts barely covered her ass.

Hell.

Those type of women didn't seem to care whose bed they ended up in—as long as it was the bed of a military man.

He'd been all about those types in his younger days but just didn't find them as tempting lately.

Didn't mean the younger guys weren't happy to take them home for the night though.

"Three points!" his team member Noah "Viper" Miller shouted, clapping him on the back. "You boys owe us a round of beers."

Mason chuckled, glancing over at the two other members of their Navy SEAL team across the blacktop. "Anytime you guys wanna pay up works for me," he said with a grin. "I could go for a couple of beers."

"Hell, you just want to see Taylor again," Jacob "Joker" Olson said, bending down to grab the basketball that had rolled to the edge of the court. He easily palmed it with one large hand, glancing up as the roar of twin jet engines temporarily drowned them out, two F-15s from the nearby naval air station flying across the sky.

"Affirmative," Mason said. "Not that I've convinced her to go out with me yet."

"She got any friends?" Jacob asked.

"The hell if I know," Mason replied, sauntering toward one of the buildings on base as the rest of the men followed behind him. "She barely said a word the last time we were at Anchors. Usually she'll hang out for a bit even if she's working. Take her time passing out drinks and grub so we can flirt a little."

Anchors, a popular bar on the Virginia Beach oceanfront, wasn't far from their Navy base at Little Creek. It was always filled with single military men and local women, both looking for a good time, but Mason had taken interest in one of the waitresses there in particular.

And his teammates had clearly noticed.

He imagined the flush that always spread across Taylor's face as he teased her when he was there with his buddies, that dark brown ponytail swinging back and forth as she moved around the bar, and those chocolate brown eyes warming up every time she looked at him.

Ryker "Bulls Eye" Fletcher raised his eyebrows, his gray eyes flashing. "Think everything's okay?"

"Dunno," Mason grunted, stalking toward the door. "She gave me her number a few weeks ago but has been busy every time I've asked her out."

"Crash and burn," Jacob said with a howl of laughter. "Guess she wasn't interested after all."

"Hell, it feels like it," Mason said, pulling open the door and flashing his ID. "I haven't seen much of her since we got back from Bogota. Maybe she thought I was blowing her off by not showing up at the bar like usual."

"She knows you're a SEAL," Ryker said. "Taylor knows the drill. We disappear for a while and then come back. Same with half of the other guys in

Anchors. No harm, no foul."

Mason shrugged as they moved toward the locker room. "Something still feels off. She was always flirty in her texts before—flirty yet unavailable, I might add."

"Shit, you've been texting her? Was she sending you fucking heart emojis or something?" Ryker asked with a chuckle.

"Very funny, jackass," Mason said as he opened his locker. He pulled his sweaty tee shirt up over his head, ready to hit the showers.

"Man," Jacob muttered beside him. "First Hunter and Colton find women of their own, and now you, too? Maybe the Delta team can have a triple wedding or something."

Their SEAL team leader Hunter "Hook" Murdock had met his girlfriend Emma in London while on the run from terrorists. Colton "C-4" Ferguson had met Camila as part of their op to take down her father, a notorious drug lord in Bogota. Neither of the SEALs had expected to fall for the women they'd rescued, but both Emma and Camila had moved to Virginia Beach and seemed happy as hell to be with their men.

And Colton and Hunter were now very much absent from their evening games of basketball and nights out at Anchors.

"I'm not with Taylor," Mason said. "I like her—so shoot me. She's gorgeous, and it's cute as hell the way she always blushes around me. That doesn't mean I'm going to marry the woman or something. Hell, I haven't even taken her out yet."

Ryker snickered, stripping off his own shirt. He balled it up and tossed it aside. "Bang her first, bro. No need to rush into marriage."

Mason muttered to himself, slamming his locker shut. The rest of his SEAL team was single and more than happy to play the field. To take home a different woman every week. What the hell did he expect? If a woman they were interested in wasn't readily available, they moved on to the next good-looking chick to come by.

No harm, no foul.

Why was he so hung up on Taylor anyway?

If she'd thrown herself at him and begged him to take her home for the night, would the thrill of the chase be gone?

It wasn't that though, he rationalized. She was different than the type of women he usually went after. More reserved. Quieter. Shy.

But something about the way she always looked at him thrilled him to no end.

If she blushed that much just from being near him, he'd love to see how she reacted if he bent over and stole a kiss. Pulled her down on the sofa at his place and made out with her.

Took her to bed and enjoyed her for hours.

"Hell," Noah said, stopping beside him, gripping his towel around his waist as he headed for the showers. "Just ask her if everything's okay. Women like that shit."

"And suddenly you're an expert on women," Mason chuckled.

"The last woman I took home didn't have any complaints," Noah quipped.

Mason smirked as his buddy walked off. Damn it all to hell. It wasn't his place to worry about Taylor, a woman he for all intents and purposes barely knew.

They were acquaintances, barely. Not friends. Not

dating. Not lovers.

He had a nagging feeling something wasn't exactly right though. And as a Navy SEAL, he'd been trained to follow his instincts. To be aware and observant at all times.

The question was, even if something was going on in Taylor's life, they were practically strangers. A few texts and flirty dinners where she waited on their table weren't exactly the start of a relationship.

Would she even want his help?

***

Thirty minutes later, Mason was driving down the highway from Little Creek toward Virginia Beach. His stereo blasted through his SUV, and the ocean breeze blew in through his open windows.

He passed a couple of large high-rise hotels, aiming for the parking garage close to Anchors.

They were at Uncle Sam's beck and call 24/7. Getting called on a mission meant they were wheels up within hours. Most of his team was still single, and they enjoyed nights out when they were all stateside. Hell, the other SEAL team stationed at Little Creek, the Alpha SEALs, were all married or in a serious relationship. A couple of them had kids already.

Mason pulled into a parking garage along Atlantic Avenue, the long stretch of road that ran along the busy section of Virginia Beach. He hopped out of his SUV, setting the alarm before crossing the dimly lit garage and walking down the block toward Anchors.

A gentle breeze blew in from the ocean. His gaze swept the area on the boardwalk—although there were a few people strolling along the water, it was nothing like the summer months when tourists flocked to the area.

He pulled open the door to the popular bar, the sounds of music and laughter and scent of fries and burgers hitting him. A long bar stretched across one side of the restaurant, but his gaze landed on their usual spot.

Hunter and Emma were already nestled at a table at the back, Emma sitting comfortably on Hunter's lap. Hunter lifted his chin in greeting as he saw Mason, his arms wrapped around his woman.

His tattoo peeked out beneath his shirt sleeve, the scruff of his beard just beginning to look shaggy, and Mason smirked at how different Hunter and his Ph.D. girlfriend were. If they weren't an example of opposites attracting, he didn't know what was.

"Where's everyone else?" Hunter asked.

"Must be busy doing their make-up or something," Mason quipped, sinking into a seat.

Emma burst into laughter, brushing her red hair off of her face. "Brilliant," she said in her British accent. "I'd love to see them in some lipstick and rouge."

"Rouge?" Mason asked, wrinkling his brow.

"The hell if I know," Hunter said, taking a pull of his beer. "Apparently it's all the rage in London."

"I'd look as white as a ghost without any makeup on," Emma chided him. "I've got fair skin that needs all the help it can get."

"You look perfect," Hunter corrected her, taking her smaller hand in his and kissing the back of it. "Gorgeous."

"Keep it in your pants, Hook," Mason said, calling him by his nickname.

Hunter guffawed as Emma's cheeks turned a rosy shade.

"Easy, princess. Mason just hasn't gotten laid in a while."

Mason chuckled as Emma shushed her boyfriend.

Hell.

Mason had been there at the London pub when Emma and Hunter had first met. The chemistry between them had sizzled right from the start. From the looks of things, it hadn't fizzled out at all since she'd moved here. If anything, Hunter was even more sickeningly sweet toward her.

Hunter.

One of the biggest, baddest dudes on their SEAL team, brought to his knees by a British chick.

"What's so funny?" Hunter asked.

"I see who wears the pants in your relationship. Emma looks like she calls all the shots. She's got you wrapped around her finger."

"Thank you," Emma said. "I always knew I liked you, Mason. Handsome and intelligent."

"Hey," Hunter said in a low voice, nuzzling her neck as she squirmed. "Don't make me jealous over here."

"Over here?" Emma asked with a laugh. "I'm literally on top of you. How could you be jealous?"

Hunter raised his eyebrows. "On top of me? Hell, I like the sound of that."

Emma blushed furiously as Mason guffawed.

Noah, Jacob, and Ryker walked in together just then, sauntering toward the back. Emma's gaze fell on Noah, her lips quirking in amusement. "I think your aviators are glued to your head. I've never seen you without them."

The men all chuckled as Noah grinned. "They do seem to attract the ladies. And don't worry—I make sure to take them off when I have a woman in my bed. Can't have them falling off during sex."

Hunter growled from his seat. "She wasn't worried—and she sure as hell wasn't thinking about you having sex."

Noah smirked. "That makes one of us. I'm already hoping to find a beautiful woman to bring home with me for the night. Just have to decide who the lucky lady is."

"Well, it sure as hell isn't your looks that draws the ladies in," Ryker said, grabbing a chair and sinking backwards onto it. "Hunter, Emma," he said, nodding at the couple.

"Where's the waitress?" Jacob asked, glancing around. "Is Taylor here tonight?"

Hunter shook his head, his eyes sweeping toward Mason. "I haven't seen her the last couple of times we've been here."

Mason frowned. "Me either. I was just saying earlier that something seems off with her. She used to be working practically every night, and she's hardly around anymore."

A young, blonde waitress walked over to their table, notepad in hand. "What can I get you boys tonight?" she asked, her pink lips shining with some type of lip gloss. Her gaze raked over Ryker, and Mason smirked.

"How about your phone number?" Noah teased.

She batted her heavily made-up eyes at him. "I'm not sure if you're my type," she teased him.

"Well, you're certainly mine," he quipped.

Hunter's gaze swept from Noah to their waitress.

"A round of beers for everyone. On me. We're celebrating tonight."

"Hoorah!" Noah said with a grin.

"Hell," Ryker said as the blonde waitress walked away. "Colton and Camila aren't even here yet."

"So we'll order them a round when they get here," Hunter said. "No reason we can't get started."

"Hey fellas," a voice drawled, and Mason glanced over to see Matthew "Gator" Murphy walking over with Brent "Cobra" Rollins. The two men were on the Alpha SEAL team at Little Creek. Both the Alpha and Delta teams worked together at times, deploying jointly on missions. The Delta team had just gotten back from Colombia though while the Alpha team had been in the Middle East.

"Where's your better halves?" Jacob asked.

Brent smirked at them. "Ella's busy taking a class. She's actually going to graduate early in December but wants to get her Master's Degree after that. She was accepted to a graduate program here."

"Hell, that's awesome, man," Mason said, nodding at the other SEAL. "To transfer schools and finish early is pretty sweet. And grad school, too? Fantastic."

Brent had met Ella down in Florida. He'd come to her rescue when her sleazy boss at the cocktail lounge where she worked had pawned her off on some men he owed money to. Ella had ended up moving to Virginia Beach to finish college here.

Such was the life of a SEAL. They went where the U.S. Navy sent them—and their wives or girlfriends had to come along, for better or worse.

"Yep. I was looking forward to seeing more of her," Brent said. "She was planning to get a job after graduating, but it looks like now she'll be spending more of her nights studying and writing papers. She's more serious about school than I ever was," he added with a chuckle.

"Bri's at home with the baby," Matthew said. "I did daddy duty the other night while some of the women went out. Now it's my turn to have a breather. Man, that little fella can scream."

"Shit," Hunter said as Emma stood and headed off to the ladies' room. "You boys could open a goddamn daycare with all the kids you have."

"Not me," Brent said. "I don't know a damn thing about babies. Nor do I want to."

Hunter chuckled. "And what does Ella say about that?" he asked, crossing his arms as he leaned back in the chair, his mouth quirked up in a smile.

Brent shrugged. "She's busy with school now—no time for a kid."

"But grad school won't last forever," Mason needlessly pointed out. "Give it a few years, bro."

"We're meeting some of the other guys here," Matthew drawled.

"Well hell, pull up a chair and join us," Hunter said. "We're celebrating our latest successful op."

"Another time," Matthew promised. He and Brent headed off to the bar area to wait for the rest of their team, and the blonde waitress sashayed back over, holding a heavy tray of drinks.

Mason's gaze landed on her name tag. "Emily," he said, watching as her eyes flicked over to him. "Have you seen Taylor around?"

"She called out again," Emily said with a wry smile, handing out the bottles of beer to the guys.

"Called out as in she's sick?" Mason asked, his eyes narrowing.

"I'm not sure," Emily said. "She's missed several of her shifts. She was sick a couple of weeks ago, but I'm not sure why she hasn't been around lately."

"Is she having car trouble again?" Mason asked. The last time the team had been in here, she'd told him how she'd paid $400 for a tow. Mason had wanted to wring the neck of the tow truck driver who'd taken advantage of a single woman. Hell, he'd have changed her damn tire himself. Now that he had her number, and vice versa, he'd hoped she'd be in contact with him more. After a string of flirty texts though, he'd disappeared with his team to Bogota a couple of weeks ago.

And he'd barely gotten a response back from her since.

Emma walked back over, her red hair swishing around her. "Camila just texted me—she and Colton are on their way."

"About damn time," Jacob said with a grin. "Why do you think they were running late? Maybe they needed some extra time between the sheets?" he asked, waggling his eyebrows.

"Hush," Emma chided him. "She just moved here. Of course they're going to be enjoying their time alone."

"Poor old Colt is pussy-whipped," Noah said, taking a swig of his beer.

Emma reached over and lightly smacked him on the arm as Hunter guffawed in amusement.

"He's pretty damn happy," Mason said, taking a pull of his beer.

"Says the guy who's been hung up on a woman for months," Noah said.

Mason shrugged. "She knows I'm interested in

her. Hell, how many times have I asked her out now? It's not exactly a state secret. First she said she didn't date customers, then that she wanted to take it slow. She gave me her number though."

"You should ring her up," Emma said in her British accent. "You have her mobile—why keep texting when you could just ask her out on a proper date?"

"I have asked her out," Mason said. "A couple of times. But you're right. I'll give her a call this weekend now that we're back in town. If she's not interested, I can take it," he said with a shrug. "But then I'll at least have an answer."

"Bravo," Emma said, as the men chuckled.

Mason scanned the restaurant out of habit, hoping Taylor would somehow appear out of thin air. The waitresses working tonight were busy, carrying full trays between tables. But as their own waitress had already said, Taylor wasn't there.

Again.

Mason clenched his jaw, reaching for his cell phone.

Now Available in Paperback!

Made in the USA
Columbia, SC
20 May 2024

35914060R00109